A NEW RACE OF MEN FROM HEAVEN

A NEW RACE OF MEN FROM HEAVEN

Chaitali Sen

SARABANDE BOOKS *Louisville, KY*

Publisher's Cataloging-in-Publication Data

Names: Sen, Chaitali, author.
Title: A new race of men from Heaven / Chaitali Sen.
Description: Louisville, KY : Sarabande Books, 2023.
Identifiers: ISBN: 9781956046021 (paperback) | 9781956046038 (e-book)
Subjects: LCSH: Travel—Fiction. | Emigration and immigration—Fiction.
Businesspeople—Fiction. | Widows—Fiction. | Authors—Fiction.
Mothers—Fiction. | Power (Social sciences)—Fiction.
Desire—Fiction. Hope—Fiction. | LCGFT: Short stories.
BISAC: FICTION / Women. FICTION / World Literature / India / General.
FICTION / Asian American. FICTION / Short Stories (single author).
Classification: LCC: PS3619.E65 N49 2023 | DDC: 813/.6—dc23

Cover design by Emily Mahon.
Interior design by Alban Fischer.
Printed in the United States of America.
This book is printed on acid-free paper.
Sarabande Books is a nonprofit literary organization.

This project is supported in part by an award from the National
Endowment for the Arts. The Kentucky Arts Council, the state arts agency,
supports Sarabande Books with state tax dollars and federal
funding from the National Endowment for the Arts.

Contents

Introduction · · · vii

The Immigrant · · · 1

When I Heard the Learn'd Astronomer · · · 17

The Matchstick, by Charles Tilly · · · 43

Uma · · · 55

North, South, East, West · · · 87

The Catholics · · · 115

A Century Ends · · · 133

A New Race of Men from Heaven · · · 151

Acknowledgments · · · 173

Introduction

The stories in *A New Race of Men from Heaven* move elegantly between the ache of loneliness and the grace of connection, however fleeting. From the opening story, I was captivated by this collection's interest in disappearances, but while the possibility of vanishing haunts these stories, I was struck just as much by their tenderness and luminous moments of unexpected discovery. The characters in this collection are frequently in motion and rarely at home in the world; they are travelers, immigrants, children who have lost a parent, adults who have lost some sense of their own possibility, would-be lovers whose romantic endeavors are plagued by hopeless awkwardness. And yet, in this beautiful book, with her gift for finding the precise language to capture a feeling, the author has made a place for all of them, a home I didn't want to leave. A lonely man on a business trip tries to write a dishonest letter to his parents while eating dinner at a cafeteria off the highway and finds himself drawn into a crisis when an unsupervised child goes missing. A widow leaves India to live with family members in whose home even the art feels "hostile to the Indian aesthetic." A department secretary is fond of her new boss and his grieving wife, Kitty, but can't change the outcome of their story or the way that Kitty disappears even in the telling. A mother who once left her family, before she herself could be left, navigates the way that even years later, when they're back together feels slightly fragile. A writer finds himself unsettled when his career is revived courtesy of an unknown impersonator. Even a sad cafeteria meal is displaced, "plucked from its home under a heat lamp." This landscape of loss and vulnerability is tinged with a quiet perseverance, full of people searching for the right way to reveal themselves, people who can find themselves briefly buoyed by the minor bliss of grocery stores and chain restaurants and crowded subway cars. Many of these stories end with a character trying to find the words to tell someone something; even the failures of language are a reminder that the attempt to put something into words is a declaration of hope, a belief that someone might be listening.

—DANIELLE EVANS, 2021

A NEW RACE OF MEN FROM HEAVEN

The Immigrant

Dhruv found this faux French restaurant off the bypass road of a highway called Research Boulevard, close to his hotel. There were many of these restaurants all over the southern and midwestern states to which Dhruv traveled for work, and he had eaten in most of them. On a Wednesday night he was having a late dinner of something they called chicken friand, a square puff pastry stuffed with chicken and peas and smothered in a thick, gummy mushroom cream sauce. As always, he ordered it from the counter and watched it plucked from its home under a heat lamp where it had been kept warm for an undisclosed length of time. This was one of the better ones, still somewhat moist and flaky. Sometimes the corners were so dry and hardened he couldn't get his fork through it, yet he took his chances on this dish every time he came.

He had to admit the concept here was well executed, a testament to the power of objects. Mounted on a brick wall across from his table, a decorative iron hook held a long-handled copper saucepan. The hook's baseplate was a pleasing silhouette of a rooster, a motif repeated throughout the restaurant, on a teacup, a ceramic jug, and a porcelain platter. A fireplace divided the two dining rooms and on the broad mantel rested a giant iron lid and a bellows. Dark wooden beams stretched across the ceiling, and some of the walls were paneled with the same coffee-colored wood. The few segments of wall not made of brick or covered with wood were accented with framed pictures—maps of France, still life paintings, and sketches of ruined castles on riverbanks. The music was baroque.

He never dined idly anymore. During this meal he wanted to get a letter written to his parents. *I am sitting in a quaint French-style restaurant,* he wrote, in English. His old friend Tuli had once joked that his parents did everything in English—they shopped in English, they ate in English, they even made love in English. Picturing Tuli's jolly, white-toothed grin, Dhruv sighed deeply before continuing his letter. He tried to describe the rustic décor and how it was meant to evoke the French countryside. This would mean little to them since neither he nor his parents had ever been to the French countryside and his parents had no appreciation for the charm of old things, no nostalgia for simpler times. They lived in India surrounded by old things, and their lives had always been relatively simple. Among the three of them, only Dhruv would have fallen victim to the manipulations of this interior. This dining room, reproduced hundreds of times in hundreds of cities, somehow awakened heartfelt pastoral yearnings, as if he'd been a French farmer in another life.

He wanted to write about a woman he loved, but couldn't

begin for many reasons. For one thing, she had not yet returned his feelings, and for another, she was Muslim, though not devout in the least. In fact, she was a heavy drinker. He believed he could fix that if she would give him the chance.

He was easily distracted from his letter. Outside in the parking lot, an old Asian man was shouting at an Asian woman, presumably his wife. Dhruv studied the man's behavior, the angry spasms of his mouth and his arms flailing theatrically under the eerie orange streetlamps. He wondered if something justifiably outrageous had set him off on a public tirade, or if he was just prone to tantrums.

Dhruv looked away momentarily to see if anyone else found this scene riveting, but the only other person facing the window was a woman sitting alone a few tables down. Dhruv had noticed her when he sat down with his tray because she was dining alone and reading a novel, and he was always curious about people dining alone. He tried to guess at her situation. She could not have been on a business trip. She was too much at home, with an unhurried air of self-possession. She looked to be in her midforties, not unattractive but not overly concerned with her appearance. His powers of deduction led him to conclude merely that she was an avid reader who had wanted to get out of her house. She did not look up to watch the man with the loose temper. Her book, whatever it was, held her unfailing attention. Every few pages she would lift her glass of white wine and take a sip, and that was her only distraction.

The Asian man threw his car keys on the ground and took off walking while his wife, somber with her head down, remained by the car. After a moment she picked up the keys and drove away. Dhruv intended to return to his letter, but his attention was once again diverted by a tiny boy wobbling around the restaurant with a giant laminated menu in his hand, smiling at anyone who was interested and tilting the menu vaguely in their direction. He was a beautiful child, with thick black hair and shining black eyes. He came to Dhruv's table.

"Are you the waiter?" Dhruv asked him.

The boy froze and stared at Dhruv's mouth as he spoke.

"Would you like to give me a menu? Is there anything good to eat today?"

He finally stood up to look for the boy's family. He did a kind of dance with him, herding him toward the adjacent dining room, where a large party had joined together many tables to accommodate everyone. An elderly gentleman saw them and came over, snatching the boy up and giving Dhruv a brief, grateful glance. As the boy was carried back to the table, he cried and dropped his menu, causing him to cry even louder and thrash about in the old man's arms. The old man quickly deposited the boy into the lap of a young woman, surely his mother. Like the boy she was strikingly beautiful, with high cheekbones and deep-set eyes. She pressed the boy's head against her chest, quieting him down, and a man who must have been the boy's father picked up the menu, while still engaged in animated conversation, and put it absentmindedly on another table. Dhruv didn't recognize the language they were speaking. Not Spanish. Portuguese? They were all dark haired and fair skinned.

Since he was up, he decided he might as well go to the pastry counter to get a croissant and a cup of coffee. He didn't want to go back to his hotel room just yet. When he returned to his table, which had been cleared of his dinner tray, he began to write what was foremost on his mind: *Ma, Baba, I have met someone.* Before he could get very far, the woman with the book made a remark. "No one is watching that boy," she said.

At first Dhruv didn't understand what she meant.

"He's wandered over here at least ten times," she said, seeming stunned that Dhruv hadn't noticed him earlier.

"Aah," Dhruv said. "Well, we are all watching him, aren't we?" He turned back to his letter, shrugging off the strange admonishment. At least he had returned the child to his family, while she sat there with her book.

As he wrote about Mahnoor, he knew he would never send this letter. He had seen her nearly every weekend for over a year through a small circle of Chicago friends who gathered frequently, yet he was at a loss for words to describe her. He listed the facts. She was a pediatric oncologist with a broad smile that turned her cheeks into two crescent moons. Long, wispy bangs grazed her eyebrows. She had a habit of brushing them aside with her fingers to reveal a narrow triangle of forehead that he found very attractive. He knew the group gathered during the week as well, in his absence, and when he returned on the weekends she always looked surprised to see him. "You're back," she would say, and he could never tell if she was disappointed or relieved. She had a distinct American accent that her friends said was a Southern drawl. *Drawl* was a word he found difficult to pronounce. She had grown up in Georgia.

Last weekend he had given her a ride to her apartment in Highland Park because she got drunk, extremely drunk, and wanted to go home before her roommate was ready. In the car Mahnoor confessed that she was thinking about distancing herself from this group of friends, that they had become too dysfunctional and incestuous, and lately she felt her life had become all about work and drinking. She needed some quiet time. She needed some time to read and travel and visit museums and learn something new, to learn how to do something new. She'd always had an interest in carpentry, in making things with her hands.

"You know," he said to Mahnoor, still thinking about the word *incestuous*, "I like to do all of those things." A rising panic threatened to strangle his voice. He did not know how he could see her if she left the group. He and Mahnoor had never done anything on their own, until this drive.

"You like carpentry?"

"Well, I've never tried it, but I have assembled a lot of Scandinavian furniture."

She laughed and laughed and laughed. He laughed too.

"I've never seen your apartment," she said. "Why don't you ever have us over?"

"I'm hardly ever there." All he could say about his apartment was that it was impressively clean. It had a brand-new kitchen that had seldom been used, and polished wood floors, and a bedroom set that matched. The walls were bare and the shelves were empty. He saw so little of it because the consulting company he worked for shipped him anywhere they liked for the workweek.

When he first got the job, he thought it would be interesting, traveling all over the country, going to business lunches, getting to know all kinds of people. He had planned to experience the culture and beauty of every place he visited, but in two years he had not seen anything but highways and business parks, and often he could not even remember where he was. The company flew him in on Monday mornings and flew him back to Chicago on Thursday evenings. Every week he was in a new city, sitting in a new cubicle in an office building that looked like thousands of others, and it didn't matter where he was, really.

"I was talking more about the travel, and the visiting museums," he said to Mahnoor, gathering the courage to ask her out on a date.

"You like to visit museums?" she asked.

"I love art. Paintings, sculpture, design."

"I would never have guessed," she said. She sounded delighted.

Once they got out of the car, she was unsteady on her feet. He stayed close beside her as they walked along the path to her building and up the stairs to her second-floor apartment. On the steps, suddenly, she stumbled and fell into his arms. She stayed there for a moment, looking up at him with her pearly black eyes, but then her eyebrows twitched and she pulled away. He was sure he had done nothing wrong. He had only held his arms out to keep her from falling down the stairs, but now that some time had passed he thought he knew what had troubled her. She had been attracted to him, there on the steps, and imagined briefly being with him before she came to her senses. The reason for her rejection was not that he was a Hindu and she a Muslim, or that she saved children's lives while he traveled around the country as a programming consultant, or even that she was beautiful and he was . . . not bad. It all rested on the immutable fact of his Indianness. No matter what he wore or how he styled his hair, he would never carry himself with the easy confidence of American men. His American-born friends taunted him about this. They told him not to be such a FOB. "Don't be fobbish," they often said, when they perceived him to be too Indian, too foreign, and he never could get what he had done to offend them.

He filled three pages of onionskin paper with this drivel about Mahnoor. He put his pen down, massaged his neck, and thought about tearing up the letter and starting again back in the hotel room, or at the airport tomorrow. He would have plenty of time in the next twenty-four hours to write a more sensible letter.

The family in the adjoining dining room was making a racket as they prepared to depart, giving him his cue that he should leave as well. They were calling out the little boy's name—Rafael—and Dhruv looked around, expecting to find the boy nearby. The woman with the book had gone. The restaurant was about to close. The heat lamps had been turned off, the counter was dark, and a girl in a burgundy apron packed the salad greens into plastic tubs while another employee brushed dust off a ceiling beam with a mop he held upside down. The dust fell, like dirty snow falling from dirty clouds, onto the food counter before the girl had finished packing away all the salad greens.

He stood up and prepared to leave, but something about the family looking for the boy, something in the volume and pitch of their voices, kept Dhruv from walking out the door. They had recruited an employee to help them look for the child in the kitchen, behind the counter, and in the party room, which the employee agreed to unlock, despite the implausibility of the boy getting into that room through a locked door. Dhruv approached the old man who had taken the boy from him earlier. "Can I be of some assistance?"

"Rafael," the man said, but his English was not good enough to explain the situation. The man called over another male relative, a boy of about twelve or thirteen who spoke perfect American English. He told Dhruv they were looking for his baby cousin. Last they saw he had slipped under the table to hide, and everyone assumed they would still find him there when they were ready to leave.

"Does he hide often?" Dhruv asked.

The boy shrugged. He did not seem as alarmed as the adults, and Dhruv took this as a good sign. He tended to trust the instincts of children, even children as old as this one, whose body language suggested this was not the first time the whole family had gathered forces to find the errant toddler. Still Dhruv was moved by the mother's panic. She had become distraught in the last few minutes and could not be comforted. Her cries were becoming increasingly desperate. She called out her son's name in a way that might have made the child feel too frightened to come out.

Dhruv decided to take a quick look outside before he headed back to his hotel room. He was not eager to become further involved in this rising drama, but he suddenly remembered the woman reading. What was it she'd said? *No one is watching him.*

Dhruv couldn't help but wonder if the woman had taken the boy somewhere, perhaps out of the restaurant but somewhere close, just to make a point. She seemed like the didactic type.

Dhruv hurried out of the restaurant and circled the building. An employee with a flashlight and another member of the family were already surveying the parking lot, which extended far out along the length of the bypass road. Behind the restaurant there were ten or twelve other shops, all connected to each other in one long concrete strip. At the far end of this shopping center there was a movie theater with a full and expansive lot. There were a million places to hide. A million places for a woman—who might be slightly mad, now that he thought of it—to take a child and still keep an eye on the scene unfolding at the restaurant. He headed for all of those places, looking around corners, columns, and bushes, out as far as the movie theater. He ran through every row of the theater lot and then ran back to the restaurant, thinking the boy must have been found by now, but as he came around the corner he saw two police cars parked by the restaurant.

When he took out his cell phone he saw that it was past eleven. They had been searching for more than an hour.

Outside the restaurant he gave a statement to the police, but all the while he imagined the interview being cut short because the boy was right there inside, slumbering in a shadow, somewhere they'd looked a thousand times without seeing him. The family was huddled together in silence at a patio table nearby. The police took a long time with the interviews and every now and then the father implored them to cut the questioning short and keep looking for his son. Dhruv tried to be quick with his details, but he wanted to be thorough. As expected, the officer was interested in the woman with the book. Most of the questions were about her, and when Dhruv was asked if he saw the woman leave, he shook his head guiltily. "I was writing a letter. I didn't notice she had gone until I heard them looking for the boy."

He heard the officer discuss the woman with his partner. "Let's hope she used a credit card," he murmured. Dhruv was a little taken aback by how firmly the woman had become a suspect based on his testimony. He hoped he had just given the facts and not misrepresented anything he heard or saw, but if the woman was innocent, the most this would cost her was a few hours of her time and some humiliation. If she was guilty, if she had indeed snatched the child, Dhruv felt at least she wouldn't harm him. He found himself hoping that his suspicions were correct. If Rafael was not in the restaurant, the best alternative was that he was with a bookish, middle-aged woman with poor judgment. Any other scenarios were far more sinister.

When he was a child, this happened all the time. Children went missing for a while until they were discovered at some neighbor's or relative's house. He himself was lost during Kali Puja when he was about five years old. He happily sat for hours with an old man who fed him sweets and told him stories. He did not even go home that night. An aunt and uncle he didn't recognize found him and took him to their house. The next morning his family's driver, Santosh, came to retrieve him, and at home he was lightly scolded for wandering off.

The officer told him he was free to go.

"I'm going back to Chicago tomorrow," Dhruv said. "Is it possible for me to get news from someone when the boy is found?"

As he put the officer's card in his wallet, he realized he had left his letter pad at his table. He was embarrassed by the thought of someone finding it and reading it, but it seemed inappropriate, petty somehow, to ask if he could go back into the restaurant to retrieve it. He said goodbye to the family and told them how sorry he was that this had happened. "I'm sure you'll find him," he said, "soon." The men shook his hand. The women bowed their heads, except for the mother, who was staring at the road, lost in a waking nightmare.

When he turned to go to his car he was surprisingly disoriented. He couldn't remember where he had parked, and although he stood for a long time staring at the silver Hyundai that was his rental car, he had been looking for his own car, parked in the basement garage of his apartment building in Chicago. Without any recollection of driving this car over the past week, he took the key out of his pocket. He pressed a button, heard the click of the car unlocking, and opened the door. He was tired and overstimulated. He would go home, not home but back to the hotel, take a hot shower, and fall into bed.

Back in the hotel room he was still awake at three in the morning. He had not even changed out of his clothes or turned out the lights. He did not turn on the television or read a book. He just sat on the edge of the bed and relived his evening in the restaurant over and over, trying to uncover something he might have missed. After a while his mind started playing a game with him, like one of those *Where's Waldo* books his nephews liked so much. Where's Rafael? He is by the fireplace. He is under the copper saucepan. He is there in the framed picture of a ruined castle.

Suddenly Dhruv covered his eyes. A rush of tears fell into his palms. His chest heaved. A groan escaped from his throat. He was sobbing like a little boy, his body expelling some kind of liquid anguish. He had never cried like this before, not even when his beloved grandmother died. He sobbed until he was exhausted. He got into bed, thinking he would fall right to sleep, but as soon as his head sank into the pillow he was restless and alert.

He took out his phone and studied his contacts list. Who could he reach at this hour? The expense on a cell phone call to his parents would be enormous and they would worry about him. He had friends in California, but it was late even for them. He came to Mahnoor's number and almost without thinking he pressed the call button. His mind was an empty vessel.

She picked up after two rings. He hung up.

His phone rang. He answered it.

"Dhruv?"

"I'm sorry. I dialed you by accident. I've woken you up."

"No," she said. "I was awake."

"Are you on call?" he asked, certain he must have disturbed something in her schedule.

"I couldn't sleep," she said. "Then you called . . . by accident. Where are you?" she asked. She sounded sleepy. He imagined her lying in her bed.

When he tried to answer he could not for the life of him remember where he was. In his mind he could clearly see the building where he'd worked that day, the on- and off-ramps of the highway, the shopping center, the restaurant, the parking lot, his hotel. This litany of images did nothing to help him recall his location. It only prolonged the silence. He thought of France.

"Dhruv?"

"One moment," he said. He looked for clues on the bedside table. There was a breakfast menu, directions for ordering movies, and even a booklet with dining and shopping options in the area, but not a city name to be found. I'm nowhere, he thought.

It came to him at last. "Austin," he said. "Austin, Texas."

He paused, wishing he had not called her, but wanting desperately to keep her on the phone. "I've had the strangest night. I was sitting in a restaurant, trying to write a letter," he began. He would tell Mahnoor everything about the missing child. But he felt mournful and guilty, overcome with an uncanny sense of anxiety, as if he were trapping the boy with his story, as if the story itself could make him lost forever.

When I Heard the Learn'd Astronomer

I could have retired after a period in which the biology department of our preeminent College of Natural Sciences split into two. I had served as the department secretary for thirty years and had already submitted my retirement papers, but I decided to stay on another year. The head of the newly formed Department of Ecology and Evolutionary Biology, Dr. Joseph Fernandes, was instantly likable and cheerfully intelligent. He was quite young and had spent the last five years abroad at Stockholm University. He seemed happy to have escaped the monotonous chill of Scandinavia. Those first few weeks, I often observed him standing by his open window, enjoying the warm, bright days.

On his desk he kept a picture of his wife, standing in front of a stone wall with a handful of tulips. A liveliness in the photograph caught my attention every time I passed it. I wondered when she would come prancing through the offices to introduce herself. In all my years as a department secretary, the wives always did this, refusing to be forgotten, even at times getting involved in controversies that had nothing to do with them. But his wife, whom he called Kitty, did not come and announce herself, and I soon learned that nothing in this small, fledgling department would happen as expected.

Early one morning, at the end of August, Dr. Fernandes stood by my desk instead of going directly to his office. He was holding one of our national newspapers, which had a reputation for fairness. "I need your help," he declared. He had already made a habit of saying this to me. "Did you happen to see this editorial in the paper?" he asked me, putting the newspaper on my desk and pointing to the article in question. It was authored by a Dr. Robert Smith of the Society for Science and Ethics. Dr. Fernandes asked if I'd heard of him.

I was surprised Dr. Fernandes *hadn't* heard of him. Dr. Smith had been making a name for himself over the last few years, on television and radio and in the newspapers. He described himself as a "lapsed scientist," though he still insisted on calling himself a doctor. I saw him as more of an entertainer than an intellectual. "A kind of professional agitator, if you will," I said to Dr. Fernandes. "No one takes him very seriously."

He waved his hand over the paper. "You mean this is a satire?"

"Well, no," I said. I did not really know how to explain Dr. Robert Smith as a cultural phenomenon.

"He completely mischaracterizes the scientific process," Dr. Fernandes continued. "He equates the teaching of evolution with religious dogma. Everything he presents as the truth is actually an inverse of the truth." His tone betrayed a kind of quiet panic.

"I was reading it to Kitty this morning and, suddenly, some things about this place started to make sense. The behavior of the. students, for example, and some of the faculty, for that matter. Does this man have influence here?"

I wanted to ask how one could possibly measure influence, or trace the source of his complaints to this one man. "Would you like some coffee, Dr. Fernandes?"

I was relieved that he said yes. I went to fetch the coffee and expected to take it to him in his office, but he had pulled a chair up to my desk and was frowning over the newspaper again.

When I sat back down, he continued to tell me about the myriad falsehoods in Dr. Smith's editorial, most notably his claim that a legitimate minority of scientists was raising doubts about the age of the earth.

"But is all this really new?" I interjected. Here I felt the advantage of my experience. I told Dr. Fernandes that in my thirty years with the department, evolution was one of those topics that had no shortage of detractors.

"Detractors?" he asked.

"Yes, you know, a student from a devout family might write a letter of complaint."

He looked alarmed. "Is that why the department broke up, because of detractors?"

There I hesitated, fearing I had misspoken. I certainly didn't have the expertise to explain why the department had split. From what I understood, Dr. Elam, who was the dean of the College of Natural Sciences, wanted the biological disciplines to have more of a professional emphasis, to prepare the students for careers in medicine and such. The split into two departments was meant to be a compromise, with the larger Biological and Biomedical Sciences absorbing most of the faculty, and our smaller department emphasizing foundational theory and investigative process.

Dr. Fernandes confessed to me that he hadn't asked many questions when he was interviewing for this position.

"I don't know how much they would have told you, anyway," I said. "I believe some of the conflict was personal."

I was present at some of the meetings to take notes, and had read and filed some of the correspondence, but when he asked me if they had discussed evolution, religion, pedagogy, truth, reality—in other words, if they had mirrored the criticisms in the editorial—I simply couldn't answer. Ultimately, the decision was made behind closed doors and came as a surprise to everyone. I don't know what department secretaries were like in Sweden, but his inflated view of my role was somewhat amusing.

"There is a pull toward agnosticism among the students that worries me," Dr. Fernandes continued. "A weak foundation in scientific thinking and, in my opinion, a fair amount of intellectual laziness."

That felt a little unkind. After all, he hadn't been with us very long.

"Perhaps there is a more rigorous style of education in Sweden," I offered.

He sat back with his coffee, silent for a moment. The halls began to thrum with activity, students going to classes and departments opening their doors. One of our new faculty arrived and commented on the editorial as well, saying he had noticed it but thought it was laughable and poorly written. After a brief exchange that left him unimpressed, Dr. Fernandes asked me, "Why is this argument in the paper? Why such a call to ignorance now? There's nothing timely about it that I can see."

"It does seem rather academic for the general public," I said.

He nodded. "Something is happening here. Something is happening." He kept repeating it, convincing himself. I couldn't have known what he meant. I might have thought he was overreacting.

He asked me to schedule a department meeting. Then he went into his office and stayed there for several hours, refusing any calls. Around midmorning, he came to me with some roughly handwritten paragraphs and asked me to type them. It was a rebuttal to Smith's editorial, giving short shrift to his philosophical argument, which he called "a cynical attempt to malign scientists." He said that apparently, these days, any fool could claim that black was white and up was down and call himself a doctor. I wondered if we ought to get approval from the college, as he was speaking on behalf of our department, but it wasn't my place to get involved in that. He had the right to publish whatever he wanted. He was defending the discipline, which was ultimately good for all of us. While I worked on getting his letter to the newspaper, Dr. Fernandes found out more about Robert Smith and his organization. These findings disturbed him even more. Hovering over my desk again, he said Smith was dangerously influential, with grand political ambitions, and this would be a disaster not only for science but for all of modern society.

His letter appeared in the paper the next day, and to my surprise, it caused an immediate controversy. I don't know that there was really an order to the incidents that followed. It felt more like the whole ceiling coming down than a series of leaks. Maybe it began with the phones ringing. I took the first angry call as some sort of prank or wrong number. But they kept coming, threats of punishment so incommensurate with the supposed offense that many of us would gather around and laugh in disbelief. After a while, we had to screen the calls and turn over the tapes from our answering machines to the campus police. The hate mail was no easier to sort through. I recruited a student to help me catalog them, but she began to have nightmares and had to stop.

It surprised me most that instead of coming to our defense, the college reprimanded Dr. Fernandes for publishing the letter without approval. He and I were both called in to Dr. Elam's office. For a few terrible years I had served as a secretary to Dr. Elam when he headed the biology department. How he made it to the dean's office was a mystery to me, but I was glad to be rid of him. He complained that Dr. Fernandes had not gone through the proper channels. He said these were not the passions they had hired him for.

I was outraged. "I take full responsibility for this," I said.

"Yes, you should have known better," Dr. Elam agreed.

"It doesn't matter," Dr. Fernandes said. "Even if she had advised me to take the proper channels, I wouldn't have complied."

This was maddening to Dr. Elam. His little mouth puckered and he had nothing to say.

The following week, six students, two boys and four girls, stormed our office to confront Dr. Fernandes. I tried to get them to identify themselves, but they would only say that they were concerned members of the campus community. They wanted to ask Dr. Fernandes some questions about his letter in the paper. Hearing the commotion, Dr. Fernandes came out of his office and offered to speak with them in the conference room, where there was more space and they could talk freely.

They refused to move, beginning their interrogation on the spot. One of the boys, with an intensely serious face and a silly haircut, claimed that everything Dr. Fernandes had said about religion could also apply to science. "In fact, isn't science just another belief system?" he asked.

Dr. Fernandes answered the question without hesitation. "Science is a process for investigating reality, based on evidence."

I wondered if he should have just hidden in his office. Everything he said prompted a new question, and it seemed we would never get rid of them. They asked him to define reality and explain how all of creation could come to be without a creator. What about evidence of the spiritual world, they wanted to know. His answers frustrated them. They asked him why he insisted on lying to students, and he said, "I'm not the one lying to you."

They all started shouting at once, and the escalating scene attracted a larger crowd, until there was no more space in the office. Soon, the small group of protesters was surrounded by students and faculty who had spilled out from the classrooms and offices on our floor. I could see the situation getting out of hand, and called security to come and help before someone got hurt. Perhaps it made things worse. The disrupters were forcefully taken out and later used their removal as a reason to claim persecution.

During a relatively calm moment after this, Dr. Fernandes tried to apologize to me. I didn't allow him to continue. It wasn't only that I felt loyal to him. I could easily be disloyal if I disagreed with his stance, but in this public and volatile situation, I felt only pride. It would not have occurred to me to temper or discourage him. I sent him away, and from then it was always to be taken for granted that I was on his side.

In the midst of all this, I had begun to wonder if I would ever see Dr. Fernandes's wife, Kitty, whom he mentioned often but never presented to us formally. I didn't meet her but by chance one morning in September, at the farmer's market. Every Saturday, I arrived before dawn to watch the pastel sunrise fill the aisles while the vendors set up their stalls. At the market, I was part of this constant motion of light and sound and people and bounty and voices, experiencing all the layers of life, all of its richness, through all of my senses. I was happy there.

I recognized her around midmorning, standing by the flower stall with a handkerchief to her nose. She loved flowers, obviously, but perhaps her constitution did not allow her to enjoy them. She turned away, sneezing repeatedly, and when she was finished, she straightened her posture with a slightly panicked expression. Her hand moved protectively to her belly, and I noticed then, with her dress pressed against her abdomen, that she was pregnant. Her dark eyes shimmered with tears. She wiped them dry as she walked down the aisle, away from the flowers. I wanted her to see me, to recognize me in return, but of course she had no reason to know what I looked like.

I caught up with her at one of the pastry stalls and touched her arm to get her attention. She turned around, and before I finished introducing myself, she grabbed my hand and cried, "It's you. I know who you are."

I blushed, wondering how she could have identified me so quickly. I knew her face well from the photograph on his desk. I couldn't quite believe I was seeing her now in the flesh, and my disbelief caused me to cackle. Kitty smiled. "I want you to come for dinner one day. I keep telling Joseph to bring me your number but he forgets."

"He's dealing with so many important matters," I said, but I didn't think she had understood the situation. I was sure Dr. Fernandes was not eager to change the nature of our relationship.

She let go of my hand and reached into her bag. She stared into it, searching for something impatiently. "I don't have a pen," she said, but I could barely hear her. "Are you all right?" I asked.

"I can't find a pen," she said, only slightly louder than before. She did not seem to want to look up from her bag.

"Please, don't trouble yourself," I said, and easily reached the pen and notepad I always kept in my purse. I wrote down my phone number, ripped off the paper, and gave it to her.

She finally extracted her hand from the bag, but it went to her abdomen again and I wondered if she was in unusual physical pain. I had no experience with pregnant women.

"Can I help with your bag? It must be heavy."

"You're too kind," she said. Tears were coming to her eyes again. She repeated that she would have me over for dinner, and I said I would wait eagerly for her invitation. I watched her hurry through the crowd and disappear.

On Monday, it was Dr. Fernandes who first mentioned my encounter with his wife. "You saw Kitty at the market," he said.

"Yes, by the flower stand," I said. "And you're . . . she's pregnant?"

He smiled. "Yes, I guess she's showing a bit."

"What good news. It must be quite a change for you."

He stared at me for a moment. Then, with some hesitation, he told me that she had been pregnant before. I knew they had no children, but still, it took me a moment to understand what he was trying to tell me. By the time it dawned on me, I was embarrassed and didn't know how to react. I remembered her hand on her abdomen, and her pained expression, which I did not dare mention to Dr. Fernandes.

I said, "I'll keep her in my prayers." It sounded entirely false. I was not an avid atheist, like him, but I hadn't prayed in years.

"How did she look to you?" he asked.

"I'm sorry?"

Then he was the one who appeared embarrassed. He put his hand up and said, "Never mind."

The students who had been removed from our office circulated a petition demanding an apology from Dr. Fernandes. They gathered hundreds of signatures, many more than the number of students in our department, and delivered the petition to

Dr. Elam's office. Naturally, Dr. Fernandes refused to issue an apology, and the college decided to hold a community meeting about the controversy, a misstep on their part. Dr. Fernandes had managed to galvanize some support among the students and faculty, and the group that had invaded our office that day was largely outnumbered. The meeting only highlighted the absurdity of the situation. When Dr. Fernandes was invited to speak, he said, "A powerful group of religious zealots is convincing our young people that there is no provable reality, that reality is a matter of opinion. Surely, our college would want to dispute that notion." One of the agitators tried to heckle him during the speech, but was quickly silenced by the audience.

Yet, despite being in the minority, the agitators didn't give up. They kept circulating their petitions and making their case. They began disrupting classes, staging demonstrations, and putting flyers up around the campus. They didn't come back into our office, but they did often gather in the lobby, where their amplified voices made them sound much more numerous than they were. Most troubling was that their numbers did grow, not by many, but enough to make us wonder if there wasn't a silent majority of them. The students on our side were not as passionate.

Even Dr. Fernandes seemed worn down by the constant activity, but he had other problems. Only a few weeks after I saw Kitty at the market, he called me from the hospital to tell me that she had lost the baby and that he would be out for a few days. He gave me explicit directions about whom to inform, and said they didn't want any visitors. I spent some time ordering flowers and almost had them delivered, until I remembered her sneezing by the flower stall at the market. I canceled the order and chose a simple card instead, which I circulated within our department and mailed to their home.

When he returned, he was no different than before. I saw people hesitating, wondering if they should offer their condolences, but he managed to discourage us without saying a word. There was no time to mourn anyway. Keeping our department alive was a consuming battle, and after a while, Kitty and her lost pregnancy were all but forgotten, though I thought about her often. Every time I saw her picture in his office, I felt unsatisfied. I wanted to inquire about her, or send her a note. It seemed wrong to treat her loss with so much austerity, but the opportunity to bring it up didn't present itself.

Eventually, some of the disruption fell away, or else we got used to a certain level of conflict and moved on. By November, we were beginning to function more smoothly. Midterm exams were given, grades were entered, and everyone—the students, professors, administrators, and staff—settled into their roles. Dr. Fernandes was invited to give a talk at an important conference and would be away for two days. He told me Kitty would not be going with him. He asked if I would call on her. She had wanted to invite me ever since she'd met me at the market. He thought this would be a good time.

She called me Saturday morning and invited me over for lunch. Before I left, I took a pill for palpitations. I don't socialize easily and worried that I wouldn't say the right things. The medicine stops my thoughts from racing, makes me better able to listen and respond in situations that would otherwise turn me mute. Indeed, I was very calm as I walked among the willows and cherry trees to the faculty apartments, sensing the whole world to be this tranquil. The leaves fluttered against a chalky gray sky. I carried a bottle of wine as a gift.

I had been to the faculty apartments often over the years, to make deliveries and occasionally help set up a luncheon or cocktail reception. They were lovely old dusty apartments. To me the halls smelled like sweet pipe tobacco. Outside of Dr. Fernandes's apartment, on the third floor, there was a tall cathedral window looking out to the university clock tower. I paused there, thinking of the first time I saw this campus when I was twenty years old. All I had wanted then was to make a home here.

Kitty opened the door before I had a chance to knock. She took the wine bottle from me and invited me into the living room, treating me as if I were a frequent guest. She looked much healthier than I expected. The only possible indications of her grief were her black dress and black cardigan.

She set the wine bottle on the coffee table. Mismatched furniture, arranged around a worn Persian rug, cluttered the living room. The walls were lined with overfilled bookshelves. In a corner nook, two leather armchairs flanked an antique end table. I imagined a couple growing old in those chairs, reading side by side when there is nothing left to talk about. It was a sharp contrast to my apartment, which was spare and sunlit, with golden walls and three large, square rooms. I could easily account for the few things I owned. I never had people over.

I accompanied her to the kitchen, where something was simmering on the stove and a pan of dough balls sat ready to go in the oven. We talked about nothing of consequence until the air was thick with the sweet smell of butter rolls. She filled two bowls with beef stew and sat us down at a small table by a window that looked out to the courtyard. I broke open a warm roll and let a bite of it melt on my tongue. Kitty said, "I wanted to thank you for the card you sent. People sent me chocolates and stuffed toys. Does that seem strange to you? What would I want with a stuffed toy? Why would I eat a chocolate after losing my baby?"

I dropped my spoon and drank some water, thankful that I hadn't sent her a stuffed toy or chocolates. "How are you now?" I asked.

Her left hand was strangling her napkin. I reached for another roll.

"My uterus is misshapen. The baby can't get enough oxygen. It suffocates in my womb. My womb is a death chamber. That's what the nurse said to me."

I doubted a nurse would say such a thing. Those had to be Kitty's words.

"It kept happening, always at twenty weeks. I thought it was Sweden, the cold, the water, the doctors. Joseph didn't want to come home, but I was unbearable."

I had not expected her to be so frank. This spilling forth of her marital conflicts put me in an awkward position.

"I thought it would be different here, but it isn't. I was born this way. My body's no good for having babies."

These difficult thoughts tumbled out of her one after the other, as if she had no control over their release. "I'm so sorry," I said.

"I wanted to have my uterus cut out. I mean, what's the point of keeping it? But they would only tie my tubes."

"It's less invasive," I said.

"See, Joseph was going to have a vasectomy when we were in Sweden. But I kept thinking, what if he could still be a father, with someone else? A Swedish woman! Men can become fathers at any age."

I took a deep breath. "I'm sure he wouldn't want that."

She nudged her bowl, still half filled with stew, away from her. "I've made you uncomfortable. Joseph says I should let people get to know me before I start talking about his balls."

I coughed into my napkin, and when I was finished I could not help laughing, and Kitty also began to laugh, to quake with laughter, at one point covering her face. I was moved by the motion of her hands, a swift caress of her cheeks as her laughter subsided and she revealed herself again, her eyes still bright and playful. I saw her as a husband might see her, an incarnation of joy.

After lunch, we went back into the living room, where she eyed the bottle of wine on the coffee table. She picked it up and studied the label. "I forgot all about this," she said. She went back into the kitchen and returned with two crystal glasses and a corkscrew. She knelt down, freed the cork, and poured wine into our glasses. There was an ashtray on the coffee table. I took out my cigarette case.

"You don't mind?" I asked.

"Of course not," she said.

She watched me light my cigarette.

"Joseph tells me you're not married."

"It's true. I've never been married."

"May I ask why?"

"I missed the opportunity, I suppose." I didn't feel like telling her that I'd had a chance to marry once, when I first came to work at the college. He was a doctoral student and would have been a good husband, kind and devoted, but hard as I tried I could not love him. After some time, he went away, and that was for the best.

"I wanted to buy you a gift," Kitty said. "But Joseph couldn't tell me what you would have liked."

"A gift? Why?"

"To thank you. For standing by him. It all sounds very difficult and I couldn't help him. I couldn't listen."

I shook my head. "You are both very hard on yourselves."

She smiled. "He admires you. He said maybe in another life, you would have been a scientist yourself."

"Oh, good God, no. He's wrong about that."

"But someone in your own right."

I thought this was strange. "I am someone in my own right, Kitty. So are you."

She demurred, but I could see she wasn't convinced.

"Tell me what you would like to do with your life now," I said. "Before you were married, what did you want for yourself?"

"I wanted to be a mother."

"What else? There must have been something else."

She didn't take long to think. "No. There was nothing. I wanted to be a dancer once, but I wasn't any good."

I gave up, realizing she had not invited me here to advise her.

"What about you?" she asked. "I don't believe it was your dream to become a department secretary." This didn't offend me. I was pleased to see this spark in her.

"All I ever wanted was to be able to stand on my own two feet. But for a while, I studied painting."

"Why did you stop?"

I didn't have a satisfactory answer. Over time, I might have become good enough to call myself a painter, but I didn't like being so hungry. "It was expensive. I didn't want the struggle."

She looked disappointed. I took out another cigarette.

"May I have one of those?" she asked. I passed her my case and lit her cigarette for her. She was tentative, but this was not her first time smoking. She stood up, walking back and forth with the cigarette between her fingers as if she were trying out another identity. All I could see now was a dancer. She stopped in front of a gold-framed mirror on the wall next to the sofa where I was sitting. She watched herself inhale, and then she parted her lips, letting the long ribbons of smoke unfurl and drift away. For the first time in many years, I had a desire to paint.

We kept on drinking and smoking. She told me she'd grown up in a strict Catholic household, one of six siblings. She was terrified all her life of hellfire and purgatory, but she had loved being part of a large family. Eloping with Joseph had been her one great rebellion. For her it was like coming out of a dark cellar into the sunlight. No one had ever told her the truth about the world before. When he asked her to marry him, she said she wanted to have many children, and he said he had nothing against children. She was happy to remember this. Her cheeks were flushed and she became animated. Suddenly, she glided to one of the bookshelves and grabbed an old book. I didn't know what she was up to until she stood in front of the coffee table and asked me if I knew Walt Whitman.

I swallowed some dread. "'O Captain! My Captain!'?"

She laughed. "No, this one. It will remind you of Joseph." She read the title, "When I Heard the Learn'd Astronomer," and recited the poem in a clear voice.

> When I heard the learn'd astronomer,
> When the proofs, the figures, were ranged in columns
> before me,
> When I was shown the charts and diagrams, to add,
> divide, and measure them,
> When I sitting heard the astronomer where he lectured
> with much applause in the lecture-room,
> How soon unaccountable I became tired and sick,
> Till rising and gliding out I wander'd off by myself,
> In the mystical moist night-air, and from time to time,
> Look'd up in perfect silence at the stars.

I couldn't remember the last time I'd listened to a poem. At first, I gathered the poet could not understand the astronomer's lecture and walked out, but in spite of that, or because of it, he was able to look in amazement at the stars in the night sky. I would have liked to hear the poem again. I didn't understand the use of the word *unaccountable*, and I don't think he actually said he didn't understand the lecture, but that he felt sick and tired, so perhaps he did comprehend it, more than he wanted to, and his body repelled it, rejected knowledge in favor of awe, insisting on an incomprehensible universe.

After she read the poem, Kitty didn't look up from the book. Just as quickly as her mood had lifted, it fell again. I told her that I enjoyed the poem, that it did remind me, in a way, of Dr. Fernandes, but she kept holding the book, staring into it.

"It's not that I can't be something else. But I wanted to give birth. I wanted to be a part of the wonder."

My heart broke for her, even if I didn't understand this compulsion. "You already are, Kitty." She couldn't see that her vitality, even in this state, was breathtaking.

She tried to smile. "You're very kind."

I prepared to leave. It was late in the afternoon and her husband would be back in a few hours. She walked me to the door and we said goodbye, but she held on to my hand. She took a deep breath and said, quietly, "Joseph doesn't tell me how he feels. He only tells me what he thinks."

This, I could see, was what she had been waiting all afternoon to tell me. I was grateful that she'd found her courage.

"Maybe he doesn't have the words, Kitty."

This seemed to make sense to her, and then she kissed me on the cheek. It had been a long time since I'd felt anyone's lips press into my skin, but somehow it was familiar enough. I wanted to return the gesture somehow, but all I could do was take my leave.

On Monday, Dr. Fernandes thanked me for spending time with Kitty. He looked exhausted by the battles of his private and professional life. I didn't want to be thanked for spending time with Kitty, any more than I wanted him to apologize for writing his editorial. On that day, after he went into his office and closed the door, I remember feeling a profound sadness that made my skin hurt. There was no relief from it, all the more so because I didn't know what had caused it.

Then Kitty appeared without warning, only a few days later. She slipped into the department while I was typing and appeared at my desk without a sound, like a ghost. I looked up, startled. She looked sick and disheveled, and was clutching some kind of parcel in her hand, tightly. I went to her right away, and when I was in front of her she fell forward into my arms and wept like a small child. Dr. Fernandes was in a meeting. I couldn't phone him and console her at the same time, but I didn't want anyone else to see her like this. I guided her into her husband's office and sat her in a chair. I knelt down and tried to get her to look at me, but she kept dropping her head. Tears from her eyes fell onto the parcel on her lap. "What happened, Kitty?"

I could see her struggling to speak. A few words came out in gasps, nothing I could understand. I took the parcel away, a thick brown envelope that bulged at the bottom, addressed to their home. There was no return address. I unwrapped her hand from my wrist. "I'll only be a minute, Kitty," and as quickly as I could I ran to my desk and called the conference room. I told Dr. Fernandes to come back, that it was urgent, and hung up the phone. I dropped the parcel and went to get a glass of water for Kitty.

I returned to her and held the glass of water to her lips, cradling the back of her head while she drank. She was exhausted, but she cried again when she saw him at the door. I stepped away and let him come. He encapsulated her, swallowed her up in his arms and allowed her, for as long as she wanted it, to disappear. I didn't realize, until that moment, that I'd never seen them together.

It was nearly the end of the workday. I left them alone and emptied the contents of the parcel onto my desk. There were at least twenty items inside, handwritten and typed letters, pamphlets, and one glossy, professionally bound booklet with a picture of a pregnant woman on the cover. It was called *Understanding Fertility*, but it was all about "three levels of barrenness"—inability to conceive, miscarriage, and stillbirth—and their causes. Miscarriages, for example, could be caused by heresy and demonic possession, from which a woman who is given to unholiness turns her womb into a death chamber, the very words I'd heard Kitty repeat during our lunch.

Someone had carefully curated this package, included psalm cards and brochures and a stack of letters, all of which were signed by people who saw no crime in sharing God's love with a grieving woman. Kitty had opened all of the letters, had read about her body, her soul, and her marriage, about her sins and those of her husband. The price of the cure was surrender.

The sun went down and the office fell dark. I turned on the desk lamp and waited for Dr. Fernandes to come out and tell me to go home. I began to hear Kitty's muffled voice through the wall, and his, less frequently. While I waited, I wrote down the names of the people who had signed their letters to Kitty. If I were a person who longed for community, perhaps I would have known some of these people. I suddenly wished to see their faces, to be able to identify them, and the ones who lashed out judgments but didn't have the courage to sign their names enraged me even more.

I don't know how long it was before Dr. Fernandes opened and closed his door softly. He came to my desk and stared at the remnants scattered across it. He had aged over the past few months. The lines on his face had hardened, but now, as he watched me gather up the materials and place them back in the envelope, he looked young again, unconfident and confused. He wasn't capable of understanding this. He asked me what they wanted. I looked up at him, and as gently as I could, I said, "They want to save her."

I put the envelope in my drawer. I would make copies and hand them to someone when it mattered. Dr. Fernandes never would ask to see it. Even he had limits to what he wanted to know, and I thought foolishly that it wasn't necessary for him to understand, that I could understand it for him, and Kitty could understand it, but we didn't need to impart our understanding to him. I now know that was a mistake.

We sat together, mostly in silence. Kitty had fallen asleep as they talked. He wanted her to rest a little longer before he took her home. After some time, he told me what Kitty had said. It wasn't the package that upset her. She said she had been fine when she left the apartment. She was coming to show it to him, and find out what he wanted to do about it.

I thought something must have happened to her on the way. Maybe she was being followed, or saw one of the flyers that had been posted around campus a few weeks back. But it was nothing like that. He explained that as she got closer, she thought about turning back and couldn't decide. She stood outside the building for a long time, and this was when she became distraught. When something that should have been easy, showing her husband a violation of their private matters, became difficult.

"When Kitty lost the baby," he said, "it was a relief to be here. To have this fight. Even if Kitty was alone. Even if she had nothing. I thought it would hurt her more if she knew how much I wanted our children to be born."

I reached across and took his hand. "You won't leave her alone again," I said. I would make sure of it. It was important to me that they not lose each other.

There were months after that, in which I loved and looked after them as well as I could, but still they left me. Joseph gave talks about a war brewing, a war of ideas that we couldn't afford to lose. He said it was science, not myth, that could best serve our need for revelation. He worked that part out with Kitty. She wanted him to inspire people, not frighten them. I remember hoping it would never go beyond a war of ideas. We weren't ready for anything else.

The night my telephone rang, I was half-awake, peripherally aware of the physical world, but I knew something terrible had happened. I thought if I didn't answer it, if it stopped ringing, then reality too would recede into the darkness. But it didn't stop ringing. As soon as I answered the phone and Dr. Elam started talking, I understood that I was alone again. He told me that Joseph was dead, that his car had blown up on the street where they lived. He had left Kitty out of the story, but of course she was with him in the car, and was also gone.

I.was picked up and taken to the office, where Dr. Elam was waiting with a list of tasks for me. I would have to cancel classes, notify the students and faculty, issue guidance from Dr. Elam about talking to the press or the authorities, and clear out the office for reasons I would not know until later. I walked away from him. He followed me and watched from the doorway as I took the photograph of Kitty and slipped it into my bag. I remained there in front of Joseph's desk as if I were waiting for his instructions. His empty chair was in the path of the faint morning light coming in through the window. I'd never seen this room at sunrise, and for a moment it felt as if this was the only thing that was different about this day. I closed my eyes, expecting only darkness and silence, but no, my head was full of voices and memories. I could have stayed there forever, but Dr. Elam demanded my attention. He had already decided to shut our department down, hoping it would stop the barbarians at the gate. It would not.

I opened my eyes, and in the shock of light I turned to him and said, "I'm ready."

The Matchstick,
by Charles Tilly

The night I found out about the story, my daughter and her husband, who is twenty-two years her senior, had invited me over for dinner at the brownstone they'd just bought in Brooklyn Heights. This was more comfort than I could have imagined for her, a three-story townhouse with an eighteen-foot coffered ceiling, the kind of place I used to linger beneath on the sidewalks of my youth, stealing views through picturesque windows of crown molding and crystal chandeliers and . . . my God, is that a wall of bookshelves with a rolling ladder? She couldn't have done it on her own, not at her age. Her husband is the director of an important New York cultural institution. I won't say the name but it begins with a *W*. She was an intern there and without any intention or effort . . . I know this deep in my soul . . . she managed to end his marriage and begin her own life with him.

I like my son-in-law. Even I can tell he's very sexy; he has a youthful sense of humor. Would I prefer to see her with someone who couldn't be mistaken for her father? Of course, if only because there is a kind of entitlement young women lose in such relationships. They forfeit the right to live without judgment, the right to fully celebrate the union. It isn't so great for me either, as the actual father. It is never far from my mind, this parasitic awareness that people look at them and blame me.

As I said, they invited me over for dinner. My daughter, looking exactly like her mother when I first fell in love with her, that autumn nymph, was absolutely beaming, so I was drinking quite a lot, bracing myself for the dreaded announcement that I was going to be a grandfather. You can imagine my surprise when she revealed the actual cause of her elation. "Daddy, I read your story in the *Paris Review*. It was stunning. I cried, Daddy!"

"Me too, Charles," her husband said. "Me too."

"Are you just getting around to reading that story?" I asked. That story was published ten years ago. Truthfully, I'd wanted to see it in the *New Yorker* but it wasn't up to me, and when it was swept up by the *Paris Review*, I was thrilled, of course. It was reprinted in *Best American Short Stories* and kickstarted the success of my novel that came out later that year.

My daughter looked baffled. "What do you mean? It was in the last issue."

I truly did choke on my wine. "I'm sorry, what story is this?"

They both laughed.

"How much have you had to drink? Your story, 'The Matchstick.' Why are you being so secretive?"

"Oh, you know," I said. That phrase has gotten me out of some pretty tight spots in my time.

"I don't think he wants to talk about it, baby. Look, he's blushing."

"Can I see it?" I asked. "I actually haven't gotten a copy yet."

My daughter bounced out of her chair like a puppy and came running back with the journal in her hand. There it was. My name in the table of contents. I went straight to the contributors' notes, where my accomplishments were listed in modest prose. There was no mention of my latest book, not surprisingly. Whoever had written this bio obviously shared the opinion that my last book was perhaps the worst piece of serious literature to be published in this century. An important cultural critic had cited the book as a symbol of our dying empire. That the novel made him think of our dying empire at all meant he'd simultaneously understood and missed the fucking point. What a feat!

I turned to the story and scanned the first line. It was not remotely close to anything I had ever written. I wondered if this had something to do with the cocaine I'd snorted, once, in the eighties. I slammed the journal shut and handed it back.

"Daddy, are you all right?"

"I'm actually not feeling very well."

"You should lie down. Why don't you stay here tonight?"

I never could say no to that little pixie face. We ate and changed the subject, and I slept as soundly in one of their guest bedrooms as if I had been on a Zen retreat.

Let me take a moment here to explain that I am not one for confessions. Somehow I find them dishonest. Perhaps it's a loathsome character flaw but I've done all right with it in the last fifty-plus years. Long ago when my wife accused me of cheating, I denied it to the end. She still divorced me but it was seemingly her fault, a choice she would have made with or without my full disclosure.

As I was walking home the next morning, vaguely recalling the previous evening, I decided to stop into a bookstore to buy a copy of the *Paris Review*. I'd let my subscription lapse a long time ago, having read little of the actual contents while I was a subscriber. I went home, put on some Mozart, and opened up to the page where my story began. Once I started reading, I couldn't stop. This was the best thing ever written in my name, and I knew where the inspiration had come from. This Charles Tilly, whoever he was, had perfectly understood what I'd been trying to do in my last novel. This Charles Tilly had done in sixteen pages what I could not do in five hundred.

Then I drank until I passed out. I spent the next several days holed up in my apartment, afraid to pick up the phone, afraid to leave. My daughter forced me out of it. She rang the buzzer obnoxiously for a good half hour one morning. Cleaning myself up as quickly as I could, I ran to the door and pretended to be surprised. "What are *you* doing here? Were you in the neighborhood?"

"We've been calling you for the last three days. What the hell is wrong with you?"

"Oh, you know, when the muse calls . . ."

She wept into my shirt. "That was really scary. Don't do that again."

"I'm sorry, sweetheart. I wasn't thinking."

After she left, I called my agent to try and get some answers, finally understanding the scale of the situation. I went to his office and for the first time since the reviews of my last book came out, he looked happy to see me. "What did you do, Charles? Everyone's talking about your new story."

"Really? Well, about that . . ."

"It sounds like you're finding your voice again. Is there a novel in there somewhere?"

I didn't know if *there* meant the new story or my head. "Did you read it?" I asked him.

"The copy's on my nightstand."

"Don't bother then, because the thing is I didn't write it."

He frowned at me. "What do you mean?"

"I don't remember writing it."

"Ok, I get it."

"No, you don't get it. You couldn't possibly get it. I know I didn't write it. I need you to find out who sent it in."

"*You* sent it in, Charles."

"I did not send it in!" I shrieked, startling us both. "I did not write that story. Call the *Paris Review* and, I don't know, see if you can get a hold of the original submission. Where did the payment go? I never received a payment. I never received any acknowledgment that they were accepting my story. Someone is fucking with me, big time."

"Jesus, Charles, you're losing it."

I pounded my fist on his desk. "Someone has stolen my identity. You're the only one who can help me. You're the only one I've told."

"All right, all right, I'll look into it. But do me a favor. Lay low for a few days, until I can find something out. Can you do that?"

He came to see me the next day with the manuscript in hand. "I put everything on hold to deal with this. By the way, they wanted to thank you again for donating your honorarium back. That was extremely generous."

I smiled, beginning to feel vindicated. "You see? I'd never do something like that. Now hand it over."

The cover letter was on top. There was an awkwardly familiar tone to it that made me cringe.

"This is not my email address," I pointed out. "And this is my old office number at NYU. There's not even a mailing address. Didn't that make anyone suspicious?"

My agent shrugged. "Maybe they figured you were homeless after your last book."

"What about the envelope?" I said.

"Are you fucking insane? They don't keep the envelopes."

I thanked him and told him I would be in touch. He was of no more use to me anyhow. I went to my computer to email myself. I composed many messages, some irate, some merely curious, but sent only this:

I am Charles Tilly. Who are you?

I waited for the reply that I knew would come. This was the design from the beginning. Someone was trying to make contact.

It came four days later.

Hello, Mr. Tilly! I am happy to finally hear from you. I apologize for the late reply. I am only allowed Internet privileges for an hour each week. Did you like the story?

I had been carrying my computer around the house like it was a crying infant. I never left its side. When I heard from my imposter, I was ready; presumably we had an hour.

At 4:24 I responded.

I would like you to know that I'm not angry, but I very urgently need to see you in person. As you can probably understand, I have many questions.

4:26 *I understand. I am afraid meeting in person would be impossible right now, for I am incarcerated.*

4:27 *Is this a fucking joke? Who is this?*

4:28 *My name is Rodney. I have been a ward of the juvenile justice system for the last two years. If all goes well (fingers crossed), I will be released in another year when I turn 18. Can you wait?*

4:30 *Listen, you little shit. If you don't tell me who you are and where I can find you, you won't want to come out.*

4:33 *Respectfully, I have done some research on this and am pretty sure I have not committed any crime. There is actually no precedent for what I have done. You have not told me if you liked the story. Have you heard anything? Has it been well received? This is my first publication.*

I couldn't write another word. The acute pain in my chest made me think I was having a heart attack, with only my computer screen as witness.

I went to see a midlevel agent in the identity theft/fraud department of the FBI. I had printed out our brief email exchange and brought my laptop, in case they wanted to examine it, but this agent was unmoved by my situation. He asked, "Did this individual take a payment that was meant for you?"

"No, actually."

"Does he have your social security number?"

"I don't think so."

"You're saying he wrote a story, and published it under your name?"

"Yes, that's what he did."

The agent tapped his pen against his temple.

"Why would he do that?" he asked.

"I don't know, sir. He is deranged, obviously."

Then the man smiled. "Mr. Tilly, if you don't mind my asking. Do you have a significant birthday coming up?"

"Yes, my sixtieth," I said, interested in where he was going with this.

He chuckled. "I wouldn't be surprised if someone's not planning a big party for you. I'm willing to bet your trickster will reveal himself then."

And what was I supposed to do in the meantime? If I didn't say anything, everyone would know, by the end of my sixtieth birthday party, the depth of my dishonesty. If I did tell the truth, I couldn't imagine what the repercussions would be. I decided to ask Rodney. I decided to ask him, "What would you like me to do?"

I sent him several emails and waited weeks for another reply. My last email was returned immediately with the message, "Delivery to the following recipient failed permanently."

My sixtieth birthday party ended up being an intimate gathering held in a room off the wine cellar of the Blue Ribbon

Bakery, a narrow, dimly lit space where the air was the color of caramel. My son flew out from Stanford to be there, and I was impressed with how much he'd matured, but I kept looking at the door, expecting other people to show up—friends, literary types—though where we would fit them I couldn't imagine. My daughter noticed the distraction.

"You didn't want something bigger, did you? You hate parties."

Where did she learn that shattered look?

"This is perfect," I said. "It's just us, then? I can relax?"

"Relax, Charles," her husband said. Sometimes I do wish he wouldn't talk.

At the end of the evening, after the kitchen had closed and the congeniality of the wait staff had long faded, I did not want to go home, to be separated from my children. I said, "You know that story I wrote?"

They nodded, expectantly.

"It was a good story, wasn't it?" I said.

They all agreed it was good.

"I just don't want to be alone tonight," I said.

My daughter took my hand, her eyes warm with pity. "No, of course not. We're all going back to our place. We wouldn't dream of sending you home alone." That's when I thought maybe I owed it to her to put the whole incident behind me, to accept it as a gift from an admirer.

Now, when I'm asked about "The Matchstick," I say I have no recollection of writing that story. This is usually enough for us to move on to my novel, which sold at auction and has been a critical and commercial success. I'm sure that when I'm dead, "The Matchstick" will be noted as the turning point of my career, when I at last figured out what the hell I wanted to say.

After my sixtieth birthday party at the Blue Ribbon, we took a taxi to my daughter's house. We had a nightcap in the kitchen and talked for a while before everyone went to bed. I went into my Zen retreat feeling warm and loved, but couldn't sleep. I lay awake terrified that I would never be able to write again. As if he might receive my message, I thought, *Rodney, my angel, if you're out there, I'm waiting.* The silence that followed was unbearable.

I got out of bed and went to the room where the *Paris Review* was tucked away on a shelf. Sitting at the desk with a legal pad and pen, I opened to Rodney's story and began to copy it word for word. When I got to the end, my hand ached, but I turned back to the beginning of the story and started again, and I did this, sentence after flawless sentence, until the sun came up and my fingers were calloused and this story, whoever it came from, became my own.

Uma

During the monsoon the leader of the Naxalites died in police custody. On one of the nights following his death, between long interludes of thunder, Uma heard shouts from the street. She got up and peered out the window to the alley but saw no one. Rain coming down like silver needles caught the light from her husband's study. As she lay back in bed she tried not to worry that the police could mark their house just from the glow of a desk light after curfew. Though it shamed her to admit it, she hoped things would settle down now. She was tired of feeling afraid.

She was drifting off when she heard the familiar sound of Baba's calloused feet scraping the tile. He blocked the light between the double doors where the edges refused to meet. A raspy hiss escaped from the bottom of his throat. As he stood there, the minor shifts of his body made a lot of noise. She heard his heel peeling off the floor, the creak of his ankle, the disgusting sound of him scratching his groin.

There was nothing legitimate he could want. He shuffled back to his room, the scuffing of his feet fading and disappearing. She went to sleep and was not awakened by Saurav coming back to bed. When she opened her eyes to the gray dawn she discovered him lying stiffly at her side. The room was quiet. The rain had stopped. For a few minutes she rested her hand on his stomach, enjoying its gentle rise and fall, until Saurav covered her hand with his.

"I heard shouting last night," she said.

"It was nothing," he answered. "Just some rickshaw wallahs arguing."

"Are you certain?"

"Yes, I saw," he said. "One owed money to the other."

"Do they not know the danger? Causing so much commotion in the middle of the night!"

If Saurav had thoughts about the two rickshaw wallahs and their shouting, he kept them to himself. Uma wanted to add, "Perhaps the worst is over," but she held back, not wanting to start a political discussion so early in the morning. Gently he returned her hand and rolled over to his side, turning his back to her. Stubbornly she crept her fingers along his shoulder blade, but eventually the calls of the waking city summoned her out of bed. The day was beginning.

A half hour later she had given Baba his tea and medication and mixed the dough for the luchis. She was too tired to roll them properly. They stuck to the rolling pin and stretched into ugly ovals with intractable appendages. Then they refused to puff and float in the hot oil. She pulled them out one by one, each more leaden than the last. She considered tossing the whole lot when her sister-in-law Meeradi charged through the door of the narrow, muggy kitchen. Despite her slight build Meeradi always overfilled a room.

"Baba is screaming for his breakfast. He'll drive us all mad." She frowned at the luchis.

Uma gave her an anguished look. "I'll start again."

Meeradi picked up the plate. "No, these are just what he deserves," she said, "but for my breakfast, do remember that the quality of the luchi reflects your depth of affection for the recipient."

Uma laughed. For Dada, Meeradi, and the girls, she mixed and fried a second batch. They were round and lovely.

Upon her return Meeradi looked triumphant. "You should have seen Baba's face. Absolutely constipated."

"That's what he gets for spying in the middle of the night."

"Filthy old man!" cried Meeradi.

"Do you think he would molest me?"

Meeradi clutched her hands to her throat. "The exertion might finally kill him!"

"Oof," Uma said, dismissing Meeradi from the room. She went back to rolling and frying luchis. The very last one was perfection, a bright full moon. She lifted it onto the plate, where it softly exhaled. This one was for Saurav.

She carried the breakfast tray up the steep stairs and cradled it in one arm while she opened the door. Saurav was tossing books into an old heavy storage chest.

"When did you drag that in here?" she asked.

He picked up another volume from amongst the various piles of yellowing books and newspapers on his desk. With difficulty she found a space to put down the tray and opened the balcony doors, letting in a burst of light and commotion.

"I can't concentrate with that incessant honking," he said.

"Hark, he speaks!" She laid her hand dramatically on her chest. "I believe he is speaking to me."

After eight years of marriage, his smile still excited her. He held a booklet they both knew well—*Make the 1970s the Decade of Liberation*. She always liked the simplicity of the first line, "The year 1969 has ended," while the next two sentences were poetic, extolling the great victories of the revolutionary masses, culminating in the exclamation "What a year it was!" She wondered if those words had tethered their revolution to a kind of nostalgia in lieu of progress. They sounded distant to her now, from another time and place that could not be revisited.

She got tired of waiting for Saurav to toss the booklet into the chest. After a moment, she took it out of his hands. "Aren't you going down to the clinic today? Dada needs you."

"Yes, later," he said. His attention was still on the booklet. She threw it behind her into the chest.

"Dada asked for you repeatedly this morning. You mustn't jeopardize our peace at home. He *is* beginning to grumble."

Even this didn't elicit an appropriate response. She knew he didn't want to talk about going down to the clinic. He wanted her to tell him there was still hope, that there were others who could lead the revolution he'd dedicated his life to in the last three years. He wanted her to tell him that he could be one of those leaders. *What a year it was!* Anything seemed possible once, but not now. She would not tell him lies.

"Look, I saved the most perfect luchi for you."

He sighed deeply and pulled her into an embrace. His head, resting against her stomach, felt unusually heavy, a contrast to how wispy he seemed lately, how immaterial.

"It's exquisite," he said. Then he released her and took a sip of his morning tea. She went back downstairs to encounter Baba's demands for better luchis. Uma obliged, but insisted on eating her own breakfast while he had his second helpings. Then she ordered him to bathe and implored him to put on the starched kurta pajama she'd laid out on his bed. He argued, as usual, but she prevailed, and only then did she have time to get ready to go to the market. Returning late morning, she entered through the clinic, off the main entrance to the house, and walked along the hallway crowded with waiting patients. In one of the examining rooms, she found her beleaguered brother-in-law swabbing the throat of a screaming child.

"Has Saurav not come down?" she asked.

Grimacing as he pulled the swab out of the child's mouth, he said, "Not as of yet."

"What nonsense," she said. "Really, Dada, you must not be so easy on him."

Uma rushed up the stairs to Saurav's study. This time she would give him a real tongue-lashing. She let the door swing open. "Saurav," she shouted. He was at the desk, his head resting on his arms, his teacup overturned and his breakfast on the floor. She stopped short, sensing something was wrong but telling herself that he'd merely fallen asleep. No matter how long she watched him, however, his body would not move. She forced herself to go to his side. When she touched him, a chill ran up her arm. She fled the room, stumbling down the staircase, where her legs were limp and useless and she could not reach the bottom. As she sat there clutching the banister and staring at the wall, the afternoon rains turned the house a dusky gray. It looked like evening but it couldn't have been later than lunchtime. Uma heard Meeradi calling for her.

When her sister-in-law appeared, they exchanged no words. Meeradi ran up the stairs past her. When she returned she tried to raise Uma to her feet. "Come with me."

Uma shook her away and covered her face with her hands. They muffled a wailing cry that seemed to be coming from elsewhere, a ghostly being in another corner of the house.

"Come, Uma. It will feel better to walk. I have you," Meeradi said. "I won't let you fall," but Uma's knees buckled and she felt monstrously heavy. She clung to the banister. Her feet always seemed to miss the landing. She wanted to get out of this blue tunnel but it went on and on until finally, with relief, she fell into a heap on the cold hard tiles. "Stay here, Uma. I'm just coming back, very soon."

Then she didn't want to be alone. Nor could she bear the thought of her husband up there, only a staircase between them. She had given up too soon. She pushed herself up to face the stairs again, but not even her gaze could reach the top.

Meeradi gave her tranquilizers and tucked her up in the tomb-like room where her nieces slept. She was groggy but could not sleep, prevented alternatively by the startling thunder and the gentle breathing, shifting, and swallowing of the sleeping girls next to her. The window was open to let in the air and sound of rain.

Later, angry voices collected on the street below. Uma held her hand over her heart listening to their escalating cries. They demanded the ejection of a suspect from his home, their rabid throaty shouts cut with the high-pitched tenor of fear and grief from the man and woman of the house. The woman's voice sounded familiar to her; it could have been her friend Lata. As she waited for some kind of resolution, knowing well how these things ended, she was gripped by a terrible clarity; her husband was dead. If the city were to erupt into more turmoil, she would have to face it alone.

She heard the mob moving on, but the damage to her nerves lingered. She wanted a stronger medicine. She rose and stumbled to the door, but even after adjusting her eyes to the light she remained on the threshold, neither in nor out of the room. Weakly she called to Meeradi, who came holding a tray and a bottle of pills. "I have brought you some warm milk," she said.

"What has happened?" Uma asked.

"The young man at the Dhar residence."

Uma had seen that boy. Saurav knew him.

Meeradi shook her head. "Who is to tell now which side is right and which side wrong?"

Saurav would have known. Uma depended on him for such judgments.

"I want to speak to Rupam." It was a sudden hunger to hear her brother's voice.

Meeradi gave her another pill and told her to drink the milk.

She drank quickly, burning her tongue and throat. Then Meeradi unburdened herself of the tray and pulled Uma forward, closing the door behind her. They linked arms and walked slowly down to the clinic, where they would sit under the fluttering lights and make the telephone call.

In the office Meeradi looked through a tattered address book filled with ant-like lettering. She lifted the enormous telephone, cradled it between her ear and shoulder, and dialed. A moment later she spoke loudly into the phone. "It's Calcutta here. May I speak to Rupam?"

Her brother's wife must have answered. Uma would not speak to her. She wanted her brother, but even after he waited on the line for her, she could not take the phone. Meeradi finally delivered the news herself, slowing down to utter the words *massive brain aneurysm* in her clearly enunciated English. Only then did Uma take the phone.

All she could remember about the conversation was that he promised to come.

Dada insisted on a traditional Hindu cremation at the Nimtala burning ghat on the banks of the Hooghly. The pregnant, humid air kept the fire from spreading as it should have, and there was an excruciating length of time waiting for the body to be engulfed. Saurav would not have wanted any of this. He would not have wanted his body to burn in public. She wished she'd had the faculties to insist on something different, for the image of Saurav disappearing under the violent flames horrified her, even under heavy sedation, until finally she fainted.

After the funeral she continued to sleep in the small room with the girls. They were a comfort to her. Baba also shifted downstairs. He took to sleeping on a cot in a room off the kitchen, where a servant once slept. Uma would often wake from her naps to find Baba patting her head or rubbing her back. She prayed that Rupam would arrive soon. It would be a great expense for Rupam to come from America, and Uma feared he would not have the money. She waited fretfully.

When her brother finally did arrive he looked so confident and healthful, so radiant, that she fell into his arms and wept. To her, he looked exactly as a thirty-two-year-old man should look, his hair neatly combed on a side part, his skin smooth and clean-shaven, and his body slim and comfortable in loose-fitting cotton shirt and brown slacks. He came in like a cleansing breeze and took her back to her youth, before she was a wife and widow.

He took her on outings, for tea and book browsing on College Street and to places he said he wanted to see again like Victoria Memorial, Birla Planetarium, and the botanical gardens, even in the rain, keeping her busy from morning until night so that she would have no opportunity to collapse into self-pity, but as the day of his departure drew near, Uma felt the suffocating heat of grief again. She begged him to stay a little longer. On his last morning, after he'd packed his bags, he sat her down at the dining room table and said, "Did I tell you that next month will be my fifth year in America?"

"It seems like ten," she said.

"It is serendipitous timing," he said. "I have applied for

citizenship and can sponsor you. I always planned to ask Saurav if he'd like to bring you."

"Saurav hated America."

"But would *you* like to come?"

"For a visit?"

"Or to stay, if you like it."

She had not expected such an invitation, and had not yet given much thought to her future. "What would I do there?"

"It's a lovely place," said Rupam. "You can help with the children, perhaps until Joy starts school, but eventually you may continue your studies. A woman of your intelligence must not throw her future away."

"Is that what you think I've been doing?"

"No, no, but now you must plan a life without Saurav. You need not lie down and wait for your death like our grandmothers did. Saurav would have wanted you to begin again, to carry on. Come to America, Uma . . . it would be so nice."

Uma noted a sadness in his voice. It was his wife who had wanted to go to America, not Rupam. Rupam had always been happy in India. "What of Supriya?" Uma asked.

"It was she who first mentioned it. She said India is no place for a widow.'"

"She said that?"

"Don't you remember that her own mother was widowed?"

The next morning, Uma woke up with that thought in her head. *India is no place for a widow.* She told him over breakfast that she would like to go to America, but she would absolutely not come unless Supriya invited her.

A few weeks later, Uma received a warm invitation from Supriya, stating that she was terribly busy and was so looking forward to having a sister in the house with her. Enclosed was also a list, written in Rupam's careful print, of nearby graduate programs in English literature that she could apply to. She gently refolded the letter and tucked it into a tin box, where she'd begun to keep her most important small possessions.

Not long after that she began to tell her friends and neighbors that she was going to America. For the next year, all talk and mental preparation was directed toward her move. She began to separate from her surroundings. It was hardest in the evenings when she relaxed with Meeradi and Dada and her nieces who begged her not to go. It was easiest when her father-in-law demanded a foot massage and seized the opportunity to rub his toes against her breasts. They finally hired a young man, with a healthy streak of assertiveness, to be his full-time attendant.

She was cleared for immigration in August of 1973. As she waited with her tearful sister-in-law at Dum Dum Airport, a middle aged émigré fell dead from a heart attack. The man lay on the floor for five hours before officials came to pick him up. Uma watched the lifeless man, dressed in a formal brown suit, and thought about her husband. She was glad to be leaving this dying country. She would soon be on a long island, surrounded by white sand beaches and ocean breezes. She imagined her nephews running barefooted, darkened by the sun, laughing on their way to the sea. How different it would be from her own cramped and sheltered childhood in Calcutta.

But as her fellow passengers gathered to board her flight, Meeradi hugged her tightly and would not let go. Uma cried, missing her as soon as they parted. The first leg of her journey was an agonizing stretch of sorrow and worry. In the air she had a heightened sense of loneliness and vulnerability. She only managed the remainder of the journey with glasses of whiskey and a set of earphones. She listened to the American pop music channel to stimulate her imagination. By the time they landed her heart raced with anticipation.

When she entered the Kennedy Airport terminal lobby, she allowed herself a moment to be impressed by the grandeur of the room and its glass ceiling, the beauty of its clean lines. It was sterile but warm, like a greenhouse or atrium. "So much nicer than Dum Dum," she thought. "Geniuses of architecture."

Then she looked for her brother among the crowd of Indian expatriates waiting for their loved ones. She was tired and over-whelmed by all the faces, and as her eyes swept over them they all looked familiar somehow, familiar yet nondescript, and so out of place in this modern facility. She worried that she might not recognize her brother, that he might not be any more familiar to her than the other young men looking out to the aisle.

She grew nervous as the crowd thinned and Rupam still had not appeared. She heard "Didi" called out several times, but never in his voice. Then she saw him, smiling broadly, rushing toward her. He greeted her with a touch on the arm and apologized for being late. Slouching and awkward, he quickly led her to the baggage claim, asking her formal questions about the flight and service, relaxing only slightly by the time they had all of her luggage in tow. Uma understood his self-consciousness. She, too, felt strangely shy.

Rupam stacked her two suitcases in the back of a long brown car that he called a station wagon. "It *is* like a wagon!" exclaimed Uma. The ride was smooth and fast. She read the large green street signs out loud—Grand Central Parkway, Long Island Expressway, This Lane Only—until she realized how irritating that might be to the driver. She told Rupam how much she looked forward to exploring the island with the children. He laughed endlessly at that.

"Why do you laugh?"

"Didi, there's nothing much to explore."

"Is the seaside not close by?" she asked.

"Not within walking. You will see that the island is rather plain."

The car slowed down as they approached his neighborhood. He pointed out the hospital, and a large building called Pathmark. "You will go there," he promised. "Truly astounding, Didi! You have never seen so much food."

When they turned onto Rupam's street, she saw neat rows of rectangular houses. The trees were quite small, with delicate, thin trunks and sparse leaves. Although Uma loved the lush, gigantic banana and banyan trees behind her husband's house, and the patches of shade that they gave to the scorching flat rooftop, she could appreciate the newness of this landscape, populated with young trees smooth and sprouting with possibility. And instead of regarding it as plain, she liked the uniformity of the street. Each house on Berkshire Road had windows and doors in the same place, with a color palette ranging from gray to white, the distance between each house just as predictable and orderly. To her, it represented the absence of chaos.

Rupam's house looked small from the outside but she was surprised at how spacious it was. It seemed to be the opposite of the massive concrete extended family homes she knew, which were so much more cramped than the majesty of their exteriors would suggest. He gave her a quick tour of the house. The front door opened into a corridor, with three bedrooms on the right and a bathroom at the far end. To the left, a wide doorway led to a long living room lit by a large window, so large it nearly took up the expanse of the front wall. The kitchen flowed from the living room. Everything was modern and clean.

"Come downstairs," said Rupam. "This is why I chose this house." He opened a door at the back of the kitchen and revealed a set of stairs descending into darkness.

"Where are you taking me?" she asked.

He switched on a light, took her arm, and guided her down. "We call this the cellar," he said. Then Uma could see why he was so excited. This *cellar* was a lovely room, with a wet bar on one side, couches and a television in the far corner, and a Ping-Pong table.

"Table tennis! I challenge you to a match!" she said.

"After dinner, let the games begin!"

As they walked up the cellar stairs, he explained that Supriya would get off her shift at 5:30 and pick up the children from the babysitter on the way home. "Babysitter?" asked Uma.

"Ayah," he explained.

"You won't be needing an ayah anymore. I shall look after the children."

"Yes, Didi," he said happily. "It will help us tremendously."

Uma took her first shower, which felt like being rained on without clothes, then changed into a new white sari. She didn't normally wear white, but she decided to dress conservatively, as this was the first time Supriya would see her as a widow. She gathered the gifts out of the suitcase and brought them into the living room, where Rupam was sitting on the couch, reading the newspaper.

He looked up at her. "Feeling refreshed?"

"Wonderful."

Rupam looked at his watch while she placed the gifts on the coffee table.

Moments later, three short honks of a car horn caused Rupam to jump to his feet. "There they are," he said. Uma dropped her bag of gifts and watched out the window as her sister-in-law slid a shiny red car into the driveway and parked it next to the station wagon.

Supriya emerged from the car, still dressed in her white physician's coat, her hair styled in neat modern layers, looking older and more angular than Uma remembered. Rupam rushed out the door, said something to his wife, and then opened the rear door of the car. Two boys tumbled out.

The first one had to be Shanti, the elder one. He was seven years old, long and skinny, followed by the short and plump tot named Joy, who was nearly three. The contrast between them amused Uma. With a bubbling euphoria she awaited the moment of introduction.

Supriya and Rupam then moved to the boot of the car and pulled out a series of bulging brown paper bags. With her nerves bursting, Uma left the window and went out to offer her assistance, but they nudged her away with a great deal of protest, refusing to hand her a single bag. Slowly they all made their way inside, with the boys leading the way. Shanti stole curious glances at Uma, while Joy studied the movement of his feet as he walked up the path, oblivious to anything else.

Back in the living room, the boys stopped and stared at the pile of gifts on the coffee table. "Are those for us?" asked Shanti.

His parents scolded him. "Is that how you greet your Uma Pishi?"

The boy squirmed under his father's reproachful gaze until suddenly, as if he'd been pricked with a sharp stick, he shot over to Uma and hugged her. Uma laughed and patted his head. "Well, of course, these are for you."

Supriya threw off her coat, dumped the bags onto the kitchen table, and emptied them at incredible speed. Rupam could not keep up, and by the time he'd put a few cans of peas away, she had completely cleared the table.

"Let me help," said Uma.

"That will be no help at all," Rupam said. "Too many cooks spoil the broth."

Uma looked back at the boys. The older one had taken a seat on the carpet, his eyes fixed on the gifts. She began to give them out, all the while distracted by the frenzy of activity in the kitchen—gathering, washing, chopping, stirring, in quick succession. Uma had never witnessed such productivity in all her life.

She gave Shanti a set of Indian comic books and a book of folktales, both written in English, and a book of Bengali nonsense rhymes. Rupam demonstrated what he must have thought to be an appropriate level of enthusiasm, carrying on about his childhood spent reading these books.

For the little one, Uma revealed a stuffed doll—a man wearing a turban and a maharaja suit. "Ahhhh," said Rupam, "the Air India man." Shanti, looking rather longingly at the Air India man, handed it to his little brother. "Look what you got," he said.

Joy was sitting with one arm slung over the edge of the couch, the other arm a mere extension of the thumb in his mouth. Slowly he reached for the doll and wrapped his stubby fingers around its leg. With his thumb still perched in his mouth, his lips tightened into a smile.

"I guess he wants it," said Shanti.

"Does he not speak yet?" Uma asked. Joy had dropped the Air India man onto his lap, already losing interest.

Uma realized her mistake only after an extended silence. The question came out as an expression of disbelief, but Uma hadn't meant anything by it. It was just that, in India, three-year-olds were such chatterboxes. They talked too much! Uncomfortably she rummaged through her other gifts, finally pulling out a sari and placing it on the coffee table.

"I hope you like the design. All the ladies are wearing it in Calcutta."

Supriya stepped into the living room. "How gorgeous," she said, then hurried back to her cooking.

Soon they sat down to an elaborate dinner of fish curry, okra, lentils, potato cutlets, and rice pulao. Supriya smiled when Uma praised her cooking. "A genuine smile," Uma thought, "makes her look lovely."

"I was planning to make biryani, but I couldn't find the time to get the ingredients."

"Oh, nonsense. Why go through all that trouble? This is wonderful."

Just then, the phone rang. Supriya sprang up from her chair to rinse off her hands and answer it. Excusing herself, she pulled the spiral cord as far out to the living room as she could, where she spoke in a calm, hushed, professional tone. Rupam explained that she was on call.

That evening, Uma and Rupam stayed up much too late, reminiscing in the cellar, playing table tennis, and drinking whiskey, which he brought out when they started talking about their favorite uncle. Chotomama, they called him. Little Uncle. He lived half the year in India and half the year in London. Uma and Rupam used to accompany him to the Saturday Club, an old colonial club that had remained much as the British had left it, except that now it was brown men barking orders at servants. There Chotomama always gave her a taste of his whiskey. He thought women should be liberated.

Rupam and Supriya spent a few days showing Uma around and getting her acquainted with the tasks that would be set aside for her. These were laundry, dusting, cooking, washing dishes, "babysitting" Joy, cleaning the bathroom and cellar, vacuuming, and keeping toys in order. Uma appreciated the modern appliances, which made these chores painless, but still she did not do them as fastidiously as Supriya wanted. After a few weeks, Supriya complained about the underwear not being folded. The next day, Uma presented her with towers of exquisitely folded underwear.

Of all her chores, Uma most enjoyed market day. On Saturdays, Rupam drove her to the Pathmark to fill her cart with whatever she needed to cook that week. It was her only regular outing. Her brother pointed out to her on one occasion that people were staring at her.

"They are probably wondering why you are dressed so formally. Why don't you wear the pantsuit I bought you?" Uma did not confess that she found pants to be the most uncomfortable item of clothing ever invented. She did not like the itchy polyester between her legs. She preferred to feel her smooth thighs rubbing against each other. Furthermore, the pants highlighted her ever so slight belly—most unflattering.

On an October afternoon, Uma and Joy sat on the couch in front of the window. Some of the leaves on the painfully thin trees had faded to yellow. She had been hearing much about the autumn colors and looked forward to the turning of the leaves, as if it would be a thunderous event. Not a sound came from inside the house, except for her nephew's gentle breathing. If the world were to end that day, she would have no warning. The stillness would just continue forever.

Uma finished washing and drying the clothes. She folded them precisely. She vacuumed the carpet, washed the breakfast dishes, and dusted the furniture with an orange feather duster. She fed Joy and prepared a snack for Shanti to eat after school. She did her morning chores slowly and deliberately, doing and redoing to make sure every speck was lifted and every corner tucked, but this only ate up an extra hour. There was still the entire afternoon to fill. She could have gone downstairs to clean the basement, or gotten an early start on dinner, but this was her daily dilemma. She wanted to be busy, but not busy with that sort of work. Domesticity for the sake of it bored her.

By now, she had read every book in the house. She wrote Meeradi a letter last week and asked her if she could afford to send her one very long, very good Bengali novel. She lamented that this was not a very literary household and most of her time was spent with a mute child.

There was nothing left to do except sleep, at only 1:00 in the afternoon. Joy lay on the couch next to her, staring up at the ceiling, sucking his thumb. Occasionally, he shifted his eyes slightly to catch her watching him. No reaction. She wondered what words, what thoughts, what pictures were behind those eyes. Those beautiful eyes. She floated in their obsidian pools, until he closed his lids and pushed her out. Rupam said they were *indeed* concerned about him, but the pediatrician assured them that he was neurologically fine, that he was simply experiencing a delay. "You know, Uma, children here are allowed to develop in their own time," he said.

What else was there to do except sleep? She sank back into the large cushions of the couch and closed her eyes.

She felt a tiny grip on her knee as Joy struggled to climb onto her lap. She helped him up and resumed her position, trying to take her mind back to where it was before it was snatched back to this couch. He laid his head against Uma's chest. She opened her eyes, distracted by his little fingers weaving in and out of her gold bangles. She patted his back, and then placed her arm around him, her hand resting on his thigh. She closed her eyes again.

She was comfortable, finally. Once she always felt like this, able to settle into rest easily, even in daylight, even with the din of the Calcutta streets filtering into her bedroom. In a house full of activity she could lay with her husband and enjoy his tongue on her breasts. Her body could accept so much then. There were no barren places, no corner that could not be touched. His hands belonged to her. She stirred slightly. Joy got tired of the bangles and moved to her necklace. She put her hand over his and held it there gently.

A moment later she sat up abruptly, nearly spilling the little boy onto the floor.

She removed Joy from her lap and wrapped her sweater tightly over her bosom. It was the sudden awareness of his fingers on her skin that alarmed her. Moments earlier she had been thinking of her husband so vividly. Joy seemed puzzled by her behavior but not disturbed. He stared at Uma for a while, then moved on to play listlessly with his toys.

She went on with her day without fully shaking her disorientation. At 3:00 she walked out to the sidewalk to make sure the school bus had arrived. She gave Shanti and Joy a snack of toast and jam, helped Shanti with his homework, and sat with the children in front of the TV for an hour until Supriya and Rupam came home. At 6:00 she served dinner and listened to them talk about the hospital.

"The dinner is quite good, tonight," said Supriya.

The compliment bothered Uma. She had been cooking for years, after all. Were dinners on other evenings not "quite good"? To avoid making a cutting remark, Uma asked Supriya what she would like to eat for dinner tomorrow.

"Up to you," Supriya answered.

After dinner, Uma asked Rupam to play a game of table tennis, but he said, "Not tonight, Didi, I'm beat." Shanti wanted to play, so they played a few games consisting mainly of Uma hitting the ball and Shanti retrieving it from the floor. His mother called down at half past eight and told him it was time for bed. "Do I have to?" he begged.

It was Uma who tucked him in and read to him from *Abol Tabol*, the Bengali book of nonsense rhymes. At the end of each poem, he asked her to read another one. That unsettled feeling she'd had all day was finally leaving her.

At 9:30, Rupam poked his head in and said, "No more stalling. Time for bed." Uma wondered why everything had to be so regimented. In Calcutta she would just be sitting down to dinner at this time. How she missed that evening chatter.

The house fell into silence, but she could not sleep.

At midnight she crept down to the basement and drank a swallow of whiskey, right from the bottle so that she wouldn't have to wash a glass. When she put the bottle down, she caught a glimpse of herself in the mirror that lined the wall behind the bar. The light was a muted orange, and it cast a flattering glow upon her face, highlighting her strong cheekbones and large, dark eyes. She had not looked at herself for a very long time. She ran her fingers along her eyebrows, then along the gentle curves beneath her eyes, over her full lips and along her jaw and down her neck, remembering caresses long gone.

The next day, after her chores, she sat on the couch again and thought about her life in India, trying to remember what she'd been busy doing all those years. She sometimes felt that Supriya looked down on her for not having children. What excuse did she have, really? Beside Saurav's ambivalence, she had her own worries about raising children in India, causing Uma to hesitate again and again. She didn't know that her opportunities would come to such an abrupt end.

Suddenly her chest tightened. She was overcome with a feeling that this house was suffocating her. She leapt up and rushed to her room, where she opened her suitcase and took out twenty of the two hundred dollars that she was allowed to bring into the country, none of which she had spent yet. She dressed Joy in his coat and hat and put her own wool coat over her yellow sari, and out the door they went. Her heart beat very quickly. She decided to walk to the Pathmark. By now she had memorized the route and felt she could handle crossing Stewart Avenue. She could pick Joy up and carry him across the four lanes. There was a grassy median in case they didn't make it in one go.

She allowed Joy to set the pace for a few minutes. He stopped to look at many things, and she would name them for him—black car, bird on a bush. He frowned at her as if she was disturbing his meditations. But when they turned a corner they both stopped to stare at something wondrous, a large tree plumed with fiery red leaves. As they stood there a generous offering fell to their feet. Joy crouched down, picked up the reddest leaf, and examined it on all sides. He then gifted it to Uma.

At that moment two boys rode by on their bicycles. By now Uma was used to the intense stares of the locals. She watched them ride away and heard the one say incredulously to the other, "Niggers." She could not hear the response. The street was empty and quiet again. Worried that they might return, she picked up Joy and hesitated for a moment, but she would not turn back now. They were only boys, she told herself. She went on toward Stewart Avenue.

When they got there, she felt daunted by the cars whizzing by. With the leaf still between her fingers, she held Joy in one arm and picked up the folds of her sari with the other. She waited breathlessly for the first break in traffic, and then lunged forward. Joy grasped her neck tightly as they ran across the street.

The running and traffic and air of adventure created a rush of euphoria. She saw a happy glimmer in Joy's eyes, too, his pudgy cheeks inflated from smiling. Safely on the other side she put Joy down and they tumbled, hand in hand, toward the store, entering through the automatic door that still amazed her. She led Joy to the aisle that she'd been dreaming of—the book aisle holding four shelves of Harlequin romances and paperback best-sellers. There she lingered, reading the backs of all of the books while Joy sat on the floor and flipped through a collection of thin

Disney fairy tales with cardboard covers. She ultimately chose a fat mystery novel for herself and *Pinocchio* for Joy. As she spent her first American dollars, she noticed that she was not thinking of India so much today. She had enjoyed the walk, and now was looking forward to bedtime, when she could lie back and read.

It was 2:30. She had plenty of time to get home for Shanti's bus if she carried Joy most of the way. She spotted a liquor store across the parking lot and decided to make a quick stop, in case she had trouble sleeping again.

When they came out of the liquor store, she picked up Joy and traveled quickly. It was difficult to carry him, the leaf, the books, and the bottle of whiskey, especially with her cumbersome wool coat. She stopped to put the bag of whiskey into her deep left pocket and gave the leaf back to Joy. The walk home seemed to take much longer. She picked up her pace when she saw Shanti's empty school bus driving past her, but she told herself that she was only a few minutes late, and that Shanti would wait for her on the stoop. He was not one to complain.

She stopped, dismayed, when she saw Supriya's car in the driveway. Not quite believing her eyes, she put Joy down and told him to run home. She continued slowly, wishing she could be hit by a car rather than face a scolding from her younger brother's wife. She had been enjoying the day so much.

Uma entered the living room and found Supriya on the couch crying, holding Shanti who was stiff and bleary-eyed. Supriya looked up, her mascara spilling into the lines beneath her eyes. "Where have you been?" she yelled. "I have been calling the house for two hours."

Joy walked over to his mother and stood by her legs. With a dramatic moan Supriya swept him up into her arms.

Uma took her coat off. "I took Joy for a walk."

"A two-hour walk, in this cold? Where on earth did you go?"

"We went to the Pathmark."

"To the Pathmark? You took my son across Stewart Avenue to go to the Pathmark? That is more than a walk, Didi. How can you be so reckless?"

Uma knew she had no authority here. She didn't answer. Supriya was now holding Joy in her lap and kissing him. "Your cheeks are frigid," she said.

Shanti looked like he wanted to be anywhere but here. Uma spoke to him. "I'm sorry you had to wait, Shanti. Were you very frightened?"

He wrinkled his nose. "Baba's late all the time." Turning to his mother he asked, "Can I go watch TV downstairs?"

"Take Joy with you," said Supriya. Joy jumped off the couch and started to follow his brother, but turned back suddenly. He ran to his coat, which was now sprawled across the middle cushion of the couch, and reached into his pocket to pull out the red leaf, a bit crumpled now. He held it up proudly. "I found it," he said in a clear but childlike voice, a voice that suited him perfectly. He dropped it into his mother's lap and ran away, through the kitchen, down the stairs. Supriya stared at the leaf, speechless.

Uma smiled. "Why do you worry so? All is well."

Supriya shook her head and buried her face in her hands. "I am so tired. Didi, do you have any idea how tired I am?"

Uma longed to be tired, the kind of tired that would make her feel like she was put on the earth for a purpose. She stood there shifting on her feet, wondering if she should sit down next to Supriya and try to comfort her. She decided not to.

Supriya uncovered her face and looked fiercely at Uma. "He was on the verge of talking. It could have happened at any time."

"Of course," said Uma.

"Do you think my job is easy? I don't have *time* to play with him and take him for walks. I wish I did."

"I know that. No one has judged you for it."

Supriya started to cry again.

"I think you're a wonderful mother," continued Uma, "and a wonderful doctor."

"Oh, for heaven's sake, what do you know about either of those things?" She pulled a tissue out of her medical jacket and blew her nose. "Your presence weighs on me."

It was true that Uma was neither a doctor nor a mother, but the biggest mystery was why Supriya would provoke her so unkindly. Now she wanted to strangle this woman.

"That's rather melodramatic."

"I am only telling you my feelings. Your brother made the decision, not me. We were perfectly happy before you came. Rupam convinced me that you would come to help. He said it would help me relax . . . I would feel less tired." Supriya squeezed her eyes shut, letting two large teardrops fall down her cheek. "But you don't make me less tired. You make me more tired."

"But what of the letter? You wrote me a letter, inviting me."

"How would it have looked if I hadn't?"

"How can you be so unfeeling? Aren't you the one who said India is no place for a widow?" Even as she said it, she realized that Rupam had lied to her.

"I never said that. My mother is a widow. She lives a fine life."

Uma felt an ache in her veins, as if air was rushing through them instead of blood. "Then," she said quietly, "I was brought here under false circumstances. It is for you to discuss with Rupam, not with me."

The silence told her that there was some truth to what she said. What sort of life would this be, being the subject of other people's disagreements? She imagined herself storming into her room and packing her bags, but her husband's home seemed very far away, and no longer a place to return to.

"I shouldn't have left the house. It was careless of me," she confessed, although it pained her to say it.

Surpriya's expression did not change at first, but in the end, she seemed satisfied with the admission of guilt. Finally she took her hands away from her face and stood up. "What did you buy, anyway?" she asked.

Uma could not believe her luck. The whiskey was still in her coat pocket. She opened the bag at her feet and pulled out the two books.

"I suppose there isn't much to read in this house. We don't have much time for pleasure reading," Supriya said. She announced that she was going to take a nap, but Uma could not let her go without one last comment. "Your son saved his first words for you. Isn't that wonderful?"

Walking past her, Supriya answered, "Perhaps I shall enjoy it after some rest."

Rupam came home just before dinner, but Uma could not face him and did not join them at the table. After the boys went to bed, he and Supriya had a hushed conversation in their room. She could not make out any of the words. Eventually they faded, and then her thoughts were too loud in the quiet of the house. She stared at an oil painting of a Rocky Mountain scene across from her bed. The painting had none of the familiar colors of warm weather places—the blues, the yellows, the oranges, the reds. She wondered why an Indian family would put up a painting that was so hostile to the Indian aesthetic. It filled her with such bitterness that she got up and took the painting off its hooks and put it down. She returned to the bed to enjoy the bare wall, but this was just as menacing. She then picked up her mystery novel but it was poorly written and she could not concentrate.

Suddenly there was a faint sound at the door. The knob was turning clumsily and she knew Joy was on the other side, his hands reaching up and struggling to keep their grip. Opening this door always gave him trouble, yet he insisted on doing it on his own. Eventually he turned the knob far enough and the door swung open. He ran in and climbed into bed with her, grabbing the only available pillow and knocking his forehead against it in a steady rhythm. He always did this when he tried to get to sleep. It was such strange behavior that she feared it would cause him brain damage. She even tried it herself, to understand the range of movements involved and assess the risks. She found that it didn't hurt at all if the pillow was fluffy, though it did put a strain on the neck and cause discomfort to the forehead. At any rate, he liked it and there was no stopping him. Uma saw him this time with a new appreciation. He came into the room with such a purposeful regard for what he wanted. He wanted to go back to sleep. He wanted to go back to sleep next to his Uma Pishi. He only expended the energy that he wished to use, no more and no less. Finally, he rested his head on the pillow, and his breathing settled, a feathery snore escaping from his tiny nose. Uma pulled up the blanket to cover his legs. She rubbed his back, and sang him a Hindi love song she used to hear in her youth.

Soja mere laal
Soja
Soja mere laal

Go to sleep
My love
Go to sleep

North, South,
East, West

The husband is still explaining it on the day of the parent-teacher conference, and the wife still carries on as if she doesn't understand. The twins will be home early, their school day shortened so their teacher can meet with parents all afternoon.

"Is the school too difficult?" she asks.

"How do I know? That's why we talk to the teacher."

Their appointment is at three o'clock, and it will take almost an hour to get there. He will be away from the shop too long. When is she supposed to start dinner? She can carry on for as long as she wants, he says, but on this he has to be insistent. This reversal of roles must reverse back. She is the mother, the one who should know the details of her children's schooling.

"It wasn't my idea to send them to a school so far away," she reminds him. "It wasn't mine either," he says.

It is true it had not been either of their ideas. It happened last year that out of the blue the twins were invited to take an entrance

89

exam to attend a new academy for gifted students. Both husband and wife bore the invitation stoically, though secretly he hoped the children would score well, thinking it would be his only achievement of late. Until then they had known their children to be odd but not particularly brilliant. They attributed their children's idiosyncrasies to other factors—twins were known to be strange, especially back home, and they had suffered a trauma when they were five years old, at the midpoint of their lives, an abandonment which was well-remembered, though none of them, not brother, sister, husband, or wife ever speak of it.

Now the twins travel by subway in the mornings with their father instead of walking with their mother to the neighborhood school. In the afternoons the boy and girl make their way back alone, instructed to come straight home and never leave each other's sides, which they never think of doing anyway. Every afternoon, they walk through the door at 4:15 and eat a snack at the kitchen table. They don't speak, except to thank their mother for the food, until they go to their room where they whisper to each other as they do their homework.

On the day of the parent-teacher conference the twins are home by one o'clock. The mother feeds them the lunch she would have packed in their lunch boxes, rice with carrots and green beans and pickled eggplant. The brother and sister eat absentmindedly, silently, each staring ahead at an imaginary theater of his and her own thoughts. The mother watches them, wondering what the teacher will tell her about her children. She is interested to know whether they are ever boisterous. A few days ago, a neighbor she dislikes asked her what she did to keep her children so quiet, a question that was at once a compliment and an accusation. The woman's own children are always shouting, always stomping up and down the stairs, and the woman herself is bombastic, thick-limbed, with oversized gestures. "They were born quiet," the wife told her. Shouting was for demanding things beyond an arm's reach. The twins always had each other, and nothing to shout for.

Their attachment to each other will be tragic one day. Already they are coming to an age when boys and girls should sleep apart, but there is no room and separating them would bring questions neither parent wants to answer. The mother wonders if they ought to split the family in half, each taking one, the two halves never seeing each other again. Would she take the boy or the girl? The boy is easier. Without his sister he might even be a normal boy, of average intelligence but quick to make friends. The girl is prickly, unforgiving, but somehow more fragile. One day she will need her mother.

"Today I'm going to your school," the mother announces. A look passes from the boy to the girl.

The girl speaks up first. "*You're* going?"

The boy is concerned. "How will you find it?"

The mother frowns. The boy notices her embarrassment and searches for something to say. "I'm glad you're going," he says.

The twins put their plates in the sink and ask to be excused to their room.

They have double homework today.

"Double homework," the mother repeats. "What is that?"

"Double, two times as much, like us."

"Double homework," the mother says again. She thinks it's ridiculous.

When the children reach their room, the girl closes the door urgently. "What's gotten into her? What a chatterbox!"

The boy isn't so surprised. Lately he sees his mother in singular gestures, an extra spoonful of ice cream, a chocolate in his lunch, a tug at his hair when she tells him he needs a haircut. He would never have admitted it to his sister but he has been waiting for this day. He still loves his mother with the insanity of a small boy, his heart still galloping every time she appears. There was a time when she went away and it stains his memory. He had willed her back with all his brainpower, and when she appeared suddenly at breakfast one morning, as if she'd only been playing a long game of hide-and-seek, his legs filled with jumping beans. He took her hands and danced up and down while she stood stiff as a lamppost, staring at him with a vacant expression. His sister had to pull him away and plop him in a chair at the breakfast table.

Later, when they were alone, she pinched him. "Can't you see that's not Mama," she said. He had to agree. His sister convinced him their mother had swapped souls with a snake. She said it was the only thing to explain her awkward movements, because a snake has no arms or legs, see? It did look as if his mother could not manage more than that, learning the use of her limbs. And she was always being watched, being held back from the children. Uncles and aunts and grandfathers came from every corner. Their own father was always clutching his head until he announced they were going to America, all of them together. The boy thought all the uncles and aunts and cousins were coming too, but they had come alone, and now the boy is the only one who watches.

Now she is going to school to find out more about the lives of her children and there is no other explanation for it but love. Snake soul or human soul, after five years she is finally learning the ways of mothers.

Later that afternoon, the husband calls her down to the lobby through the intercom. In a moment she appears at his side. He opens the door for her and she gives him a polite glance on her way out, as she crosses into the November gloom. The day is cold, the first cold day of autumn. Wind blows the withered leaves off the trees and churns them around the courtyard. When they reach the sidewalk, a breeze lifts her hair and he is surprised by her earrings.

He asks if she is warm enough. In the apartment she is always overdressed, armored from head to foot in flannel and wool, but out here her legs are bare except for a sheer layer of pantyhose. She is wearing a skirt and pumps with a low heel, items he has seen in the closet that were never moved, never touched, as if they belonged to a departed loved one and were kept like relics in a shrine. Her covering is a thin raincoat tied with a belt around her waist. He thinks she's dressed too formally for a parent-teacher conference, but her effort is endearing and he wants to tell her she looks lovely. He doesn't dare say it. If he acts as if he has any right to offer his approval, she will likely turn back. She says she is warm enough and they leave it at that.

At the subway entrance, he descends ahead of her, though she stays close behind him, and when he pulls two tokens out of his pocket she takes one confidently. The last time he saw her use the subway she was hesitant at the turnstiles, pausing too long after putting her token in the slot and furrowing her brow as she shuffled forward. She didn't so much walk onto the platform as allow herself to be tossed ahead with a slap on the bum from the turnstile. She looked back at it, scowling at the offense, and then she scowled at him. He had not realized he was laughing.

This time she passes through it with much more grace and they head toward a wooden bench, scarred with doodles scratched into the surface. She sits and examines the markings and he leaves her there. He has a bad habit of standing too close to the edge of the platform, where he cranes and stares into the black mouth of the subway tunnel, waiting for the beacon of an approaching train.

They had not grown up with anything so efficient as this. When they were young they used to squeeze themselves onto a crowded city bus to get to and from school. Before they were ever lovers he'd gained an intimate knowledge of her maturing body from those bus rides alone, but even before that, they had often been physical in their play, like lion cubs.

They had lived on a street so congested they couldn't see anything beyond the edges of the flat rooftops. Sometimes they looked up, when rain was imminent, when the clouds were especially amusing, or later, when the sunset turned the sky peach or the moon passed over them. One day when they were around seven years old, he caught her looking at the sky with a longing he had mistaken for something else. He seized her and kissed her hard, crushing her little bud of a mouth. Immediately she pushed him off and punched him in the chest, wiping fat tears from her eyes. Many years later he said, I'd like to kiss you but I'm afraid you'll punch me. He had that line in his head for a long time before he used it. She kept him waiting with the sweetest of smiles before she closed her eyes and offered her lips.

That was his first betrayal. She couldn't have known all the things troubling him during that kiss, which he had asked for but not wanted. He was thinking of a different girl, one he met after he left home, at a university in a northern hill station where the sky was a creamy blue. That girl was unfamiliar and extraordinary and they were passionate from the start, perfectly matched in all of their sensibilities. He had wanted a quick marriage after his schooling was finished, but he had no money, no status, and her family wouldn't agree. In a moment of petulance, he broke it off with her, choosing instead someone he thought to be his equal, someone who knew his worth. He failed to see any harm in marrying a girl who was like a sister to him.

Years later, when the tedium of his life caught up with him, he found his lost love. They spent an afternoon together as if no time had passed, and it went on like that for a while until they realized neither of them could bear this life. Every goodbye felt like a needle in his heart. They made plans; he would leave his wife, she would leave her husband, they would go abroad, erasing the history that had kept them apart.

He feels the train coming, a surge of warm air and dust, before he sees the glow of a headlight. The light thickens before the train bursts into view. For a brief time, hatching dreams with the woman who had become his mistress, his future was exactly this—a broadening light, an advancing train. He steps away from the edge of the platform and looks back at his wife, who is standing now, clutching her handbag and coming to meet him in front of the sliding doors. They wait as a few passengers step off the train, and when the way is clear they enter the train and separate again. She chooses a seat by the window and looks out even though there is nothing to see as the doors close and the train burrows back into the tunnel.

Standing nearby, with his hand wrapped around a pole, he sways with the bends of the tunnel and watches his wife, knowing she won't turn away from her window. He wonders what she is thinking about, if in her mind she is still standing at the edge of the ocean, staring at the sunset. He found her like that once, on a beach resort far from their home, a place she had read about in a women's magazine. It was three weeks after he told her he was leaving her. Initially she had taken the news well. She had said she understood, that she wanted nothing more than for him to be happy, that they would be lifelong friends, and the next day she vanished. She left their young children at school and failed to turn up that evening, or the evening after, or after. The police said she must have jumped off a bridge and drowned in the river, and that was what everyone wanted to believe, that she had been driven mad by the end of her marriage. She would not have left her children for anything but inconsolable grief, but she did leave her children for less than that—a picture in a magazine, a glossy dream.

At their stop he calls to her and puts his hand out, as she imagines he does with the twins who might race to take his hand. She stands up and leads him off the train. "That way," he says, pointing to the exit that will put them on the right side of the street. When they emerge at street level, they are at the bottom of a canyon, the sheer walls of the skyscrapers pulling their gaze up to the heavens. The school is several blocks to the east, close to the river, in a prewar neighborhood away from the towers of midtown. The traffic thins, the sky opens, and they come upon a brick structure built in 1908, once utilitarian in its form but now a thing of great beauty. In the front of the U-shaped building, in the scoop of the U, there is a concrete playground with climbing equipment and children's games painted onto the ground, jumping games, ball games. The lobby is cavernous, leading to things in all directions, an auditorium, a cafeteria, and two stairwells. They have to climb the stairs to the fourth floor, and then wait in a blue hallway for the teacher to open her door. Many parents are waiting, sitting in small plastic chairs or pacing silently, looking at the work stapled along the walls. The ceilings are high, perhaps twenty feet high, and above each classroom door a glass panel carries sunlight into the hall from the classroom windows. The hallways are wide, allowing for an easy flow of children, of children but also their games, their language, their ideas, and their emotions.

The wife wonders what it must sound like during the school day, all those voices and footsteps, and the teacher's voice rising above them. She is curious about all the classrooms, their arrangements and the materials provided. Even before the twins were born she'd taken a keen interest in child development and read Dewey, Piaget, Erikson, and Maria Montessori. She spent years observing the subtle signs of growth in her children, reporting things to their father that he missed when he was at work, their attempts at conversation, their charming misuse of a word. She was always decoding the logic of their choices, deconstructing the mechanisms of their miraculous brains. Then he would ask her something absurd like, "What did they eat today?" as if her only job was to feed them.

Outside their classroom, there is a display of a research project called "Cities Around the World." The girl has written a paper about Alexandria, *the pearl of the Mediterranean*, and the boy, oddly, chose Minsk. The wife begins to read his paper while the husband hovers next to her, interrupting her reading to offer a translation. "I can read it," she says. Surely he knows she can read English, slowly but competently. Certainly she can read a child's paper. Reading a language and carrying on a conversation are two different things, and she was always more of a reader even in their own language. He walks away. She can see his feelings are hurt. She goes back to her reading. The story of Minsk begins at the end of the last ice age, with the carving of the ancient river valley of Urstromtal. The boy is a storyteller. He likes to begin at the beginning. The girl's paper is more precise, more focused. Perhaps she had more creative ideas but was afraid to try them.

At last the classroom door opens. Another mother and father come out, who recognize the husband and nod their greetings. The teacher appears in the doorway and extends her hand to the husband. They have met before. He shakes the teacher's hand and introduces the two women. The teacher speaks to the mother as if she'd just come out of a long convalescence. "It's so nice to see you," she says, and the mother, fixated on the emphatic *nice*, forces a smile in response.

The teacher has an artistic look about her. Her many layers of clothing seem to have no beginning or end. She invites them into the classroom and they all sit around the table as if someone might bring them coffee and biscuits. The teacher pulls over two piles of work, one for each child, and the mother, seeing all the work, thinks this meeting will go on for a very long time. "Can we take it home?" she asks, meaning the work, and both the husband and teacher stare at her, either startled by her voice or misunderstanding the question. Perhaps her pronunciation is worse than she thinks.

The teacher turns to the husband to reply to the question. The husband looks at his wife and translates. The work stays in the classroom. Some will be sent home at the end of the year and some will go into a portfolio, which they get upon graduation from the school after eighth grade, in four more years.

Four years! the wife thinks, almost laughing. They're ten-year-olds, not architects.

Not yet anyway, though the first project the teacher shows them resembles architectural drawings, on large grid paper, of famous skyscrapers. Notes in the margins turn out to be mathematical facts about the buildings, their height, width, slopes and angles, numbers of windows, even the volume of bedrock that was dug away in order to create the foundation. The teacher hurries through the other samples and then leans back in her chair. She begins to talk again, rambling about the children. Sometimes she pauses so the husband can translate. She says it has taken a while for her to get to know the twins, because they are quiet and speak mostly to each other, but in the past few weeks she feels they are opening up, speaking up more and initiating conversation with their teachers and peers. The teacher struggles to convey her recent interactions with the twins, and the mother notices a film of moisture forming in the teacher's blue eyes. The blue of her eyes is translucent, like the shallow part of the tropical ocean where you can see right to the sandy bottom. She says something about a museum trip and the girl staring at some paintings, the teacher having trouble tearing her away from the paintings when it was time for them to go. The girl had said something to her in the museum, the meaning of which eluded the mother and even the father who didn't bother to translate. The teacher put her hand on her heart, which must have been nursing this tender memory of the girl in the museum. She uses the word *extraordinary*. The teacher asks the husband, "Do you have a translation for that word? Extraordinary?" The husband looks appalled, and the wife jumps in to save him. "I know the meaning. Extraordinary," she says, pronouncing it perfectly, she thinks. It cannot be translated. The closest word she can think of means *without equal*, and that is not close enough.

"I don't need to show you all this," the teacher says, pointing with a tilt of her head to the work still left in the pile. "You know who your children are. They're extraordinary."

The husband asks if they play with other children. She stumbles over a long explanation that the mother interprets to mean they do not actually play at all. They used to have arguments about the twins playing. He complained that she didn't allow them time to play, and she said they were always playing, all day. What did he think they were doing over there with the blocks? They played with everything, empty boxes, rocks, cups, bracelets. Their room was full of tactile treasures. He had wanted them involved in sports, at the recreational clubs in which children as young as three were introduced to field games like hockey, football, and lacrosse. He enjoyed them when he was young, but all she remembered were lashings from the other girls if she fumbled and lost a game, which she often did. She couldn't believe the things he chose not to remember. Outside of the recreational clubs they roamed around the neighborhood, a band of unruly children. To him this was freedom; this was a joyous childhood. He didn't remember being trapped by some older boys who paraded him around the neighborhood with his pants down. He didn't remember the old man who stood on his balcony calling them cockroaches and the children pelting him with pebbles. There were so many things he didn't remember.

The meeting ends, but as they walk away from the classroom, something feels unresolved. The mother lingers in the stairwell, watching her husband bounce down the stairs. Sometimes, from the back, he is still like a little boy, the way he walks, slightly bowlegged, and the way he tackles staircases, leaping down, running up, as if the thing waiting for him at the top or bottom is some wonder he'd never seen before. He stops on the landing and looks up at her. "Are you all right?"

"Wait for me outside," she says.

"Is something wrong?"

"There's something in my shoe, that's all, or else I'm not used to them."

He doesn't budge. Sometimes on melancholy days when she didn't want to play he would wait for her, refusing to leave until she agreed to come outside. And he is still here, when he should have been nothing more than a childhood memory, he is still here. Why had they done it, she wondered. When they announced their engagement, she had not received any heartfelt congratulations. Everyone knew something she didn't, though no one had warned her. No one had discouraged her. She didn't want to marry a stranger, but a stranger was what she got.

To prove her point she sits down on the top step and takes off her right shoe. There is nothing in it, but she shakes it upside down and pretends to drop a pebble from it.

"I know they get it from you," he says, ignoring the problem of the shoe. She would like to know exactly what he means. Does he feel their strange manners come from her side of the family, or is he acknowledging her efforts when the twins were young, before their troubles began?

"They don't play," she says, reminding him of their arguments long ago.

"It doesn't matter. They're happy."

The teacher had not said they were happy. She is certain of that.

"Wait for me outside," she says. She wants him to go. The stairwell suddenly feels too narrow for the two of them, and obligingly he turns the corner. His footsteps reverberate, echoing, until a door opens and shuts again, and she is alone on the empty stairwell.

Outside, she finds him slouching with his arms crossed. This is his idle pose, when he is bored, when he is waiting. She tells him she's ready and he looks up, asks her if her shoes feel all right. She says yes, they're fine, and they walk slowly toward the subway. It's cold and late. The day is fading. When they get down into the station, too many bodies have already filled the platform. He nudges her forward, like a needle along a hem, hooking her elbow with his hand as the train approaches. She thinks about her children making this journey by themselves, the crowd spreading like a bruise, pushing them along the platform.

The husband plows her through the crowd until they are on the train. More and more people behind them want to board and the wife has not felt herself so roughly handled by strangers since her own school days. The doors try to close a few times. They close and open again, close and open again. People shimmy in, out of the doorway, and finally the rubber edges of the doors come together and seal. The train moves in fits and starts and bodies are thrown together into an awkward intimacy. There is nothing to look at but the frayed fibers of her husband's blue sweater. She is as tall as his chin and can feel his soft exhalations in her hair.

When they come out of the subway, the wife wants to stop at a nearby greengrocer. At the grocer's he is supposed to leave her and continue toward the market street where his electronics shop is well situated in the middle of a busy block. He watches her pass the stalls of fruit under the awning but loses sight of her once she is inside. On the weekends they all go to the supermarket together to get everything they need, the four of them walking home with grocery bags in their hands, but sometimes during the week she claims to run out of things and has to come here. Often, he thinks of the people he knew in another country, another life, and wonders what they would think of his life here. Would it look to them like something they had once imagined, once predicted for him? He hoped not. He hoped they had imagined something better.

Even after his wife has said goodbye, he stays outside the greengrocer and waits, anxious for her to come back into view. Every day he thinks of the woman he gave up and wonders what he would do if he were to see her again. In five years, their lives would have become widely divergent. They were two people who never should have known each other. If he saw her again today he would not know how to present himself. He might find he still loves her, but now he knows there are desires stronger than love.

He can't remember all the things he said to his wife when he found her by the ocean. He must have said her children, who were blameless, were suffering, that all of her devotion to them had been undone. The boy did nothing but cry and the girl was a quiet mystery, and he had been preparing to take them abroad, where they would have a new mother, where there would be more children, and after some time the twins would barely remember her, their real mother. He tried to frighten her with this threat of losing them forever, and he also begged her to come home, to stop punishing him, because he would stay. He would stay and try to love her the way she deserved to be loved. He tried to show his rage, pity, and regret all at once.

But nothing he said had any effect on her. Shaking her head, smiling tenderly, she said it wasn't her wish to punish him or the children. She only realized that she no longer wanted the things she had been told all her life to want. She did not want to be a mother anymore, or a daughter, or a sister, or a wife. She wanted to be a woman who lived by the sea and nothing more, and short of kidnapping nothing could make her get on a train with him to start over.

He had no choice but to return home without her. Her brother asked him if he was a man or a cunt, and he said, if you can do better, go ahead, even knowing as he said it there would be no more redemption after that. The moment he told her brother where to find her, he knew something unforgivable would happen, something to follow them for the rest of their days. Her brother was the one to bring her back.

The wife squints at him as she comes out with a single bag. "You're still here," she says. He sees the bag sagging heavily with onions and potatoes and takes it from her, saying he will walk her home. He thinks their meeting with the teacher has been unexpectedly successful, and her engagement with the world surprisingly swift. He is proud of her and flushed with admiration as they walk home in silence. In their lobby, at the bottom of the stairs, she says, "I think I can make it from here." Her tone is light. She wants him to say goodbye but all he wants to say is *forgive me, forgive me, forgive me.* He drops the bag at his feet, his hands trembling, and when she comes forward to retrieve it, he stops her, putting his hands on her shoulders. He wants to say something to her. He wants to tell her he can't believe she is here with him, the little girl who taught him how to love, and didn't she agree this was no life to be lived alone? But all of that is too much to say.

There is a commotion at the door. She pulls away and watches as their neighbor noisily enters the lobby. Of all the people to come upon them, this woman is always invasive, always causing a scene. She approaches without hesitation, smiling libidinously. "Are you going up or coming down?" she asks. "You've lost an onion."

The wife hurries to pick it up. She puts the onion in the bag and grips the railing, preparing to run away up the stairs.

The neighbor gestures gallantly. "After you."

The wife is halfway up the stairs before he finds his voice. "I have to go back to the shop."

"Yes, all right," she says, without looking back.

The neighbor leans in close. "I didn't mean to interrupt. I know how it is, with children and all."

She does not know how it is, not for a second, but he gives her a guilty shrug and she remains pleased with herself.

For a long time, the wife sits alone in her bedroom. In this room, because there is no other available, she and her husband have learned to keep their bodies still and tight, arms in, legs straight. He only comes to bed to sleep, only after he is so tired he can't stay awake. She has always been a light sleeper. When he comes to bed it wakes her and pushes her to the edge of the mattress.

There is a knock on the door. The boy. He asks, "Are you here?"

"I'm here," she answers. She asks him if he needs something.

"No," he says, but his feet are glued to the floor.

"I'll be out soon," she says. He stands there a few seconds more, then shuffles away. That boy. He never did give her up.

Through the walls she can hear the twins talking to each other. She takes off her shoes and her coat, puts on her slippers, and leaves the bedroom behind her. Being alone in it has not helped her. She looks out at the small apartment, the narrow kitchen and cheap dining table just big enough for four, the living room with a couch and two armchairs, the television her husband watches with the sound low every night before he comes to bed. Within this little space she ought to know her children better. They ought to know her.

She knocks on their door and opens it without waiting for a reply. The twins and all their papers are spread out on the floor. They are working on different things, the boy on his writing, the girl solving math problems. She does not often see this room with the twins in it. After they go to school she tidies the room every day, folding the clothes they throw on the floor, dusting, vacuuming, remaking their beds. She often wonders why. It is such a feeble way to live one's life.

The twins sit up, surprised to see her standing in the doorway. "Not finished with double homework yet?"

The boy smiles. The girl looks confused.

The mother sits down on the girl's bed and invites her children to sit across from her, on the boy's bed. They come and sit close to each other, facing her expectantly.

"Did the teacher give a good report?" the girl asks.

"Of course," the mother says. "Your work was very good." The boy and girl give each other congratulatory looks.

"Next year, maybe you will go into different classes. Now that you're growing up."

They nod, already resigned to their inevitable separation.

"Not that we don't want you to look after each other. You should always look after each other." The mother closes her eyes for a second. Her nerves are threadbare. "You might remember that I had a brother, but he never looked after me."

She cannot tell if they remember him or not. He used to entertain them with stories and tricks, but they were instinctively wary of him. It satisfied her to watch them reject him, to know they recognized the monster behind his clownish disguise.

"What was I saying?"

"You had a brother," the boy reminds her.

"Yes. I had a brother. We weren't like you. All my life I wanted to get away from him."

"Is that why we came here?" the girl asks, her eyes alight. "To get away from him?"

"Yes," the mother says, relieved to have a reason. In truth she had not been a part of that decision. By the time her husband announced they were leaving, she had long realized her life was not her own. It likely had nothing to do with her, and everything to do with the woman he loved, from whom there was no escape distant enough.

The boy has tears in his eyes. Even the girl looks warmly at her. The boy and girl clasp hands. She sees so much of their father in them, and none of herself. When she was returned, first to her childhood home, then to her husband's, her brother said he had saved her from her selfish impulses, that she would never again think of abandoning her children.

He couldn't have guessed she was going to come home on her own. She had wanted to come home and tell her children, one day when they were old enough to understand, that she'd only seized a chance to be free once in her life, only once, drunk on salt water, by the sea where she was gloriously alone and unmolested. If her husband had waited a few more days before sending her brother after her, she would have returned. She would have taken her children somewhere new, to raise them without him. But her brother came for her. Her brother, a cousin, and two others she remembered from his turbulent youth. She ran, trying to lose them in a crowd before they caught her and dragged her to her brother's car. Her brother drove and her cousin watched from the front passenger seat as the other two carried out her sentence. It was a long ride back to the city where they lived.

When she physically recovered and her brother kept coming around with his bloated triumph, she asked him if she was the only one to blame. Didn't her husband deserve a lesson as well? In front of her brother she listed her husband's crimes. He had taken a mistress. He had planned to run away with her. He was probably planning to run away still, now that she was back with the children. That same evening, her husband was dropped on their doorstep, barely conscious. She knelt beside him but couldn't tell if he saw her clearly. He was smiling strangely, mut-tering something unintelligible. For a moment she wondered if he thought she was the other one, and then, not knowing what else to do, she kissed his blood-filled mouth.

She wants to explain herself to her children, whose hearts are so open. At sunset, the sea was golden and taut across the horizon, and filled with love for lonely people. If she had taken them with her, perhaps they would still be there now.

When their father gets home, he comes to their room to tell them he has brought home a cake to eat after dinner, because he is proud of them and they deserve something special. The girl shares this with her father, an epic love for sweets. Every day on their way to school, a European bakery with cream-filled pastries entices and sometimes ensnares them. The cake has not come from there, it has come from a place closer to home, but their father assures them this cake causes legendary attacks of euphoria all over the neighborhood. The twins hug their father. The girl hangs on a little longer, because it has been a strange day and she is sad and happy at the same time, and she wants the comfort of her father's embrace.

She tries to imagine what the teacher could have said to make her parents so breathless. They are like a painting suddenly com-ing to life. A few weeks ago, the class had gone to a museum, which had once been the mansion of a wealthy industrialist. There wasn't enough time to see everything, and the tour only highlighted a few portraits of important people, but the girl liked the paintings of people in the middle of their lives, a man and woman talking by the window, a girl reading with her dog curled at her feet. When they came to paintings like that she always lagged behind. Each one for her was an entire world, a book you could read in a fraction of the time, and she resented being pulled away before she could experience enough of it. The teacher kept an eye on her, allowing her to follow at her own pace, but when it was time to go it was time to go. "Maybe your parents can bring you on the weekend," the teacher suggested. The girl shook her head. "My father is working. My mother doesn't leave the house." She felt a little guilty for exaggerating. The teacher put her arm around her and the girl relished the pity.

"What do you look for in the paintings?" the teacher asked her. "Is it something in particular?"

The girl had to think about it. "I'm looking for the story."

"Yes," the teacher said. That part seemed to be expected.

"And the painter. In each painting I think there is an object, a person or animal that represents the artist."

The teacher was skeptical. "Why do you think that?"

"Because that's what I would do if I could paint. I would paint myself somewhere into the picture, but in disguise."

She didn't know if the teacher understood her, but she nodded with great sympathy and took her gently by the hand.

Her mother calls them to dinner. The four of them sit in their usual spots at the kitchen table, mother and father facing each other, brother and sister facing each other too, north, south, east, and west. Her father is always the focus of attention at dinnertime. This is his time to ask questions and catch up with their school day. They have to furnish many details to keep him satisfied and with every answer he seems to reevaluate his whole life.

But today their father does not ask them a single question. Apparently, his day has been more interesting than theirs. He took their mother across the river and something mysterious happened. The girl can feel it, this honeyed secret that caused her mother to come into their room and their father to eat his dinner with silent distraction. As if things weren't strange enough, their mother begins to talk about cities, telling them what she learned about Alexandria and Minsk, and they all watch her, listening like she is some kind of prophet. When she was little, she says, she read a book about Baghdad. Baghdad was a walled city with four gates, named for the cities to which they pointed. Kufa. Basra. Khurasan. Damascus. She loved the sound of that list, four gates, four cities. They were a prayer in her head. Whenever she wanted she pushed all other thoughts away just by chanting their names.

They seem to have a power over her even now. She doesn't dare repeat them again. She looks down at her plate and the girl sees she has not eaten very much. She has only talked. She wants to tell her mother to eat. That's what mothers do. They eat.

Suddenly there is a terrible shriek from across the table. Her brother has burst into tears. "What's going on?" he cries. "Is someone dying?" Their father pulls him over with one sweep of his arm and holds him like a toddler on his lap. How embarrassing, brother sobbing like a baby against their father's chest. Their father's face is flush with repressed amusement. There is laughter in his eyes while her brother wails and shakes. He glances across the table at their mother, not really at their mother but at someone he loved before them. She is smiling a little, only a little, but beautifully.

"Is it time for cake?" the girl says wearily.

Her mother looks at her, inhales her. Her smile widens and the girl is wobbly with a feeling that has no word. Not joy. Not love. She thinks but it is useless. There is no word for it and all she wants is a piece of cake.

She hardly has to wait a minute. Her mother gives her the first piece. Her brother wipes his face and goes back to his seat. Her father asks if they have finished their homework. Their forks clink against their plates. The girl says the cake is delicious. She is waiting for an attack of the euphoria.

The Catholics

Sharmila and Laurie spent the Obama years renovating a blue two-story on Chestnut Street, a tall, narrow house with a covered front porch flanked by two giant pines. It was built in 1910 and had only one bathroom when they bought it. A steep slope down to the street made the path treacherous and presented a landscaping challenge. They weren't able to solve the problem of the slope but now their house had two bathrooms and an extension off the back where they built their master bedroom.

They debated over moving so far from Cornell, which meant they would have to drive to work in their one car, but they couldn't find anything affordable closer to campus. This was a mixed-income neighborhood with a small complex of rough-looking apartments further down the street. Next door to them was a charming red colonial which they'd thought to be as old as their own house, but according to the records it wasn't built until 1989. When it went on the market in 2016, they had tried to get Pete and Mario, their close friends from New York City, to buy it as a second home in the country. They weren't interested, and the people who ended up moving in were Catholic hipsters with seven children, going on eight. The father, Dave, was some kind of freelance computer guy and a drummer in a band. The mother, Kiki, was a long-limbed waif with a belly so swollen it was nauseating. They had their own live chickens and traveled in a school bus, painted sky blue.

Sharmila and Laurie had watched from an upstairs window as the blue bus rolled into the driveway and the brood of children burst out of it.

A few days later, they went over to introduce themselves to Kiki and Dave and their small army ranging in age from fourteen to two, not including the one in utero. Kiki gave them a tour of the property. The kids were polite, not in a creepy way, and their little four-year-old girl was particularly cute, but the many eclectic and colorful crucifixes going up on their living room wall raised some alarm bells. If it were not the twenty-first century, Laurie and Sharmila would have assumed that they were liberation theologists or something like that. But to be so stubbornly averse to birth control these days was suspiciously right-wing.

When they got home, Sharmila said Dave and Kiki were probably Trump supporters.

"Really? They just don't seem like the type," Laurie said.

"They're totally the type," Sharmila said.

Growing up in Brooklyn, and then spending her adult life among artists and academics, Laurie would not have had as much opportunity to encounter conservative hippies, but Sharmila grew up in Waco—a hellmouth of megachurches that vomited up Chip and Joanna Gaines (exhibit 1), Christian fundamentalists who dressed just like Dave and Kiki. Ostensibly they remodeled derelict houses on HGTV, harmless enough, but in reality they propagated a patriarchal domestication cult that Sharmila was convinced would bring on the apocalypse.

They started referring to the family next door as *the Catholics*. The kids, loud and raucous and doing fun things in the backyard, were homeschooled by Kiki. From the upstairs windows, Laurie and Sharmila could observe their progress on a large airy chicken coop, an elaborate multistory playscape, and a lush vegetable garden. Sometime in mid-September Kiki had the baby, which she kept strapped to her body as the rest of the kids swirled around her. Sometimes they caught her looking up, maybe at Laurie and Sharmila in the window or just at the sky. They hardly ever saw Dave, who went more often out into the world, even after the baby was born. Once Laurie and Sharmila spotted him on the Commons loading his drums into a bar for a gig. They looked at each other with matching grimaces of disgust. Whose life came to a halt to raise eight kids? Not his.

Nothing seemed to change for them after Election Day. Kiki and the kids were in the backyard continuing their work, building a veritable fortress of innocence and ignorance. On Inauguration Day, Laurie and Sharmila didn't watch the news. Instead they drove to the city to pick up Pete and Mario and continued on to DC for the Women's March, a communal event unlike anything they'd ever experienced before. That night, Laurie raised a glass at dinner and said, "This won't take four years!"

Back in Ithaca, Sharmila remembered Laurie's prediction as they watched the Muslim ban protests. With renewed hope, they watched the people defying the post-9/11 sanctity of airports, the lawyers hunkering down with their laptops, all the signs and footage circulating over Twitter and Facebook saying immigrants and refugees were welcome, and so soon after the inauguration! If there was a silver lining to Trump's election, it was that the people were awakened. It was the people who would stop Trump, very soon, before he could even get started.

Their optimism was tempered by a simultaneous and unnerving sense of doom. Sharmila worried about her students at the LGBT Center. It weighed heavily on her that this could be the only safe space these students would have for the next four years. And Laurie coped with her grief by sitting in her office and trying to meet the deadline on her biography of Jacob Lawrence; her progress was slow, as she felt utterly useless and self-indulgent making a career out of art history. In contrast, the Catholics were always outside, claiming the open air with their hammering and laughing and running around.

The only thing Laurie and Sharmila looked forward to was a visit from Pete and Mario, who usually came up to Ithaca once a season and had long planned a trip for the end of February. To get ready for the visit, Laurie cleaned the house and got a fire going while Sharmila made osso buco and apple tart. Pete and Mario would sleep upstairs in the guest room next to Laurie's office. Sharmila never claimed a room upstairs, since she already had a perfectly good office at the LGBT Center, but if Laurie's office door was open, it meant that Sharmila could sit in there while Laurie worked on her book. There was an armchair set up just for Sharmila, where sometimes all she would do was drink her tea and stare out the window at the view. She was in love with the geometry of this region, the line graph profile of the horizon, the sharp points of the trees, the dips and waves of the hills and valleys. Right from their house they could see the great unfurling of the Allegheny Plateau. She got the same euphoric feeling here that she got in New York City, rooted in her relief and gratitude that this was not Waco.

Pete and Mario got a late start leaving Manhattan and reached Ithaca around nine o'clock, bringing a case of wine in along with their suitcase. They quickly settled in to their old ways, as if they'd gone back to a year before all this, when they all felt as if they'd chosen to live their lives in accordance with their epoch, a time of progress to which each of them were making a small contribution—Laurie with her scholarly work, Sharmila with the LGBT Center, Pete with his curatorial vision, Mario . . . Mario was a corporate lawyer working on acquisitions and mergers, but as the son of a postal worker and a bus driver, his success provided tangible benefits for his family. They talked about art, about work, about the weather and every few minutes there was something that threw them into fits of laughter. After dinner, they cozied up in front of the fireplace with their glasses of wine and slices of apple tart. They tried to watch *Mad Max: Fury Road*, which they thought would keep them awake but didn't.

The next morning, everyone was in a good mood. As she made a pot of coffee, Laurie remarked that she'd had so much fun last night, she'd almost forgotten who was president.

"Me too," said Mario. "I don't think his name came up once. It's like we called a moratorium."

Pete said, "Man, fuck that guy."

But this broke the moratorium. Once they mentioned the unmentionable, they couldn't let it go.

"Trump's too stupid to be that much of a threat," Mario offered.

"It doesn't take a genius to burn down a house," Pete said.

"But it's the whole regime!" Laurie exclaimed, "It's a vicious cabal!"

The boys cracked up. "Who talks like that? 'Vicious cabal'?"

Laurie laughed with them. "It's true though!"

After breakfast, Laurie and Sharmila took Pete and Mario to Cornell for a look around. They stopped at the art museum, a modern building next to the architecture school that always reminded Sharmila of a Polaroid camera. Laurie wanted to show Pete a participatory installation called *Empathy Academy: Social Practice and the Problem of Objects*. Students in the art department would be adding their own contributions to the exhibition later in the semester. Laurie loved the idea of a living exhibit and she wanted to curate a show like that with Pete one day, but Pete couldn't conceive of when or where that would be possible. At the moment, he was a curatorial project assistant for the Whitney Biennial, a freelance position that Laurie had helped him get. She had connections because right out of undergrad she had worked for a brief time at the Whitney, back in 2001 during the last big national disaster.

They had lunch at a new farm-to-table restaurant downtown, then went home for some quiet time. Pete was disappointed that it wasn't snowing. They always hoped for snow on their winter visits, but snow was not as reliable as it once was in Ithaca. Some years it was still abundant, but this winter was a disappointment. Old-timers could remember when it snowed from the end of October to the beginning of April. Then, suddenly the trees would blossom and a short spring would zip straight into a long, hot, humid summer. A fresh snowfall sculpted Ithaca into something magical, but there would be no chance of that this weekend.

While Mario worked on a brief and Pete went into Laurie's office so they could talk about her book, Sharmila combed through recipes on Sam Sifton's blog, *What to Cook This Week.* She hoped Pete would give Laurie the motivation she needed to finish that damn book. Laurie had a virtual vault full of research, interviews, and digital photographs, and had developed a close relationship with several members of Jacob and Gwendolyn Lawrence's extended family. Laurie owed it to them to get this story out into the world, but Sharmila gave up trying to speed things along. Every time she nudged, however gently, Laurie would have a panic attack and stop writing for days.

Early in the evening, Sharmila was in the kitchen pulling out ingredients to make a roast chicken with wild mushrooms. If this house were nothing but the kitchen, Sharmila would not mind. It was huge, even larger than what she was used to in Texas, fitting a long solid wood farmhouse table that the rest of the house, with its tight corners, could not have accommodated. The kitchen was chic and rustic, modern and vintage, masculine and feminine. It was the last room they did after months of deliberating, finally settling on white quartz countertops with black custom cabinets, dark oak flooring, red brocade chairs, and one magnificent crystal chandelier over the table.

Mario came in, opened a bottle of wine, and watched Sharmila arrange a tray of soft cheese, sliced baguette, and olives. This was the first Pete and Mario visit in years that Laurie and Sharmila didn't have people over for Saturday dinner. All of their friends in Ithaca loved Pete and Mario. Some of the wealthier liberal types went on too much about how genuine and fun and uncomplicated and "authentic" they were. Laurie and Sharmila did not feel up for all that this time, and even Pete and Mario had said they just wanted to watch movies and relax.

Yet this cheese tray cried out for a more festive atmosphere. The house felt too quiet, too dark. True to form, Mario figured out how to lift the mood. He paired his phone with Laurie's surprisingly robust little speaker and blasted their dance song "Single Ladies (Put a Ring on It)" by Beyoncé. Sharmila and Mario had been practicing the moves to this song for years now. The music shook Pete out of his slumber and Laurie out of her office. Now it felt like a party, and everyone remembered that this was a weekend for fun and happiness. Sharmila could remember them all dancing like this in their tiny apartment in Washington Heights. She couldn't believe how young they were then, and how lucky she was to have found love so easily.

During dinner, they were mellowed by the wine and Sharmila's succulent chicken and Ella Fitzgerald playing on the speaker. It had been such a perfect day. Then they cleaned up and sat on the couch to binge-watch the Aziz Ansari show *Master of None*.

They were each annoyed by something different yet no one was in favor of stopping it.

"He is so not sexy," Laurie said.

"His pining after white women is so boring," Sharmila said.

In the middle of the fifth episode, someone rang their doorbell. It was past nine, later than they'd ever had unannounced visitors. Laurie and Sharmila went together to the door and saw Kiki standing there, jumping up and down in a parka, perhaps in some kind of trouble. Immediately, Laurie swung the door open.

Kiki smiled and said "Sorry to bother you" with utmost cheer. For once there was no baby hammocked to her chest. The temperature outside had dropped and a blast of cold air flew into the house. "Come in, come in," Laurie said.

"Is everything okay?" Sharmila asked. Kiki looked so young without her kids, like a college student.

Kiki noticed Pete and Mario in the living room and waved at them. The boys waved back, looking intensely curious and somewhat amused, as if they'd been waiting for something unexpected to happen.

"Do you need something?" Sharmila asked. She was not raised to be rude to visitors but she tried to put a little clip in her voice. They'd successfully avoided the Catholics for months now. She could not believe their streak was coming to an end on their one weekend with Pete and Mario.

"Umm, what am I doing here? Argh, mommy brain. Oh, I was wondering if you have anything for a headache? I'd drive into town, but it's so late and Dave's not here."

"Sure," Laurie said. "What are you allowed to take?"

"Just over-the-counter stuff. The usual."

Laurie vanished down the hallway to go look in the master bathroom. Pete and Mario emerged from the living room, like animal cubs coming out of their dens. Mario was empathetic and hospitable. "Are you not feeling well? Do you want a drink? A glass of wine?"

"She probably can't have a drink if she's nursing," Sharmila said.

Kiki rushed to say, "I can have a little."

"It'll help you with your headache," Mario said. With that absurd statement, Mario and Pete were co-conspirators. Kiki was marched to the kitchen, seated at the head of the table, and given not only a glass of wine but some French bread and Brie cheese and grapes. She took off her parka, which Pete whisked away to hang on the coat rack.

"Wow, I haven't been this spoiled in forever. Are you some kind of angels?"

"So where's Dave?" Sharmila asked.

Kiki washed her bite down with a glug of wine and explained that Dave was in Europe on tour with his band.

"Is he famous?" Pete asked.

Kiki laughed. "I love the way you've done this kitchen."

Just then Laurie appeared, unfazed by the domestic scene at the dinner table. She set down Tylenol, Advil, Aleve, and Motrin. Kiki took two Motrins and smiled at everyone, incredibly alert and lively. She kept fixing her eyes on different parts of the kitchen, the backsplash, the range, the cabinets, the chandelier.

"Dave's in Europe," Sharmila announced for Laurie's benefit.

With more prompting from the boys, Kiki began to talk about Dave's tour, what kind of music he played and where he was at the moment—Amsterdam.

Pete interrupted. "I have to ask you, your man is in Amsterdam and you are in Ithaca New York, with . . . you have kids, right?"

Kiki blushed. "Yeah, I have eight."

"No!" Mario exclaimed as if he were hearing this for the first time. "You don't look like you could have eight kids."

"Thank you," she said, "But I do. Ocho."

"*Ocho niños, dios mío,*" said Mario.

"That's actually what Dave calls our baby. Ocho."

"Doesn't it bother you that he gets to be in Europe while you're stuck here with all your kids?" Pete asked.

"I could have gone if I wanted to. I could have left my kids with my parents and just taken the baby. But why would I want to leave my kids? They're cool people. I like hanging out with them."

You're not hanging out with them now, Sharmila thought. Kiki went on to say that her oldest was fourteen and helped a lot, that the baby was sleeping but could sleep until three or four in the morning now. She also said the wine and food and Motrin were really helping her with her headache. By then, they all had glasses of wine. Mario took out his phone and asked if Dave's band was on Facebook.

"They're more on Instagram," Kiki said, sharing their handle, which Mario was able to pull up easily. There was a band picture that he passed around, Dave and three other hipsters in wool hats sitting by a canal in Amsterdam. Pete asked her details about the kids. Names, ages, did they go to school? Kiki explained that she was homeschooling them. When Pete asked her why, she said she thought school was too confining, too institutional. She wanted her kids to be free to explore things at their own pace. If she had any objection to a public, secular education, she didn't express it here.

"Can I ask if you did this kitchen yourselves? It's amazing."

"We did most of it ourselves," Laurie answered. "We hired people to pull up the linoleum and install hardwood."

"God, I hate the linoleum. I started pulling it up myself but now there's just a big sticky mess in the corner of the kitchen."

"I can give you the name of our guy."

"I'd love to get a tour of the house one day. We're planning to renovate next summer."

"Why don't you show her the house now?" Pete asked. "You don't have to rush back, right?"

Kiki clapped with delight. "I would love that."

Laurie and Sharmila were both raised to keep their house ready for company. They both knew it would have been rude to say no.

Laurie led the way, with Pete, Mario, and Sharmila trailing behind. Kiki relished the tour, taking her time in each room, asking about fixtures and colors and where they got their ideas from. When they got upstairs to Laurie's office, the least orderly room in the house because the walls were covered with photographs and prints and notes, Laurie explained that she was working on a book about Jacob Lawrence. Kiki's enthusiasm seemed genuine, though she admitted to not knowing who Jacob Lawrence was. "Who writes an actual book, that's fucking awesome!"

She went to a different set of pictures on the opposite wall, a triptych that Laurie was writing a paper on for the Arts in Society Conference in Paris. The first picture was a close-up of a group of white people turning their gaze to their right toward the camera, sometime in the 1920s. A different version of that picture could be found on the internet, revealing in the background the charred body of a Black boy hanging from a tree. The next picture was from Nazi Germany, a crowd of thousands on what seemed to be a sunny day, tens of thousands, facing a stage punctuated with towering outsized swastikas. The final photograph was from a Trump rally, resplendent with reds and whites and blues and the rapturous florid faces of his supporters looking at their savior.

Kiki looked closely at the pictures, peering into each one for a long time.

"What do you think of those?" Sharmila asked.

Kiki exhaled. "I mean, yeah, I guess, God, this is so intense."

For a minute no one said anything. The question of Kiki's politics went conspicuously unanswered.

"Well," Laurie said, "that's the house."

"It's awesome. Your house is beautiful."

They all went back down the stairs. At the bottom, Sharmila planted her feet by the front door. Kiki got the hint. She said she'd better get home before one of her kids woke up and called the cops to file a missing person's report. She grabbed her parka off the coat rack. But just as Sharmila opened the front door and Kiki stepped toward it, she stopped and faced everyone.

"I don't know who needs to hear this," she began. "This may be way out of line. But my heart is telling me just to come out and say it." She put both her hands over her heart for a brief pause, making eye contact with Laurie and Sharmila. "I just see that you two are so stressed out all the time and I hate that you feel like you have to worry so much. You're so lucky, you know, and your lives are so great—I mean you made this life that's so great. No one can take what you have away from you. No one!"

Sharmila smiled and opened the door wider, but Laurie stopped Kiki from leaving. "I'm not sure I know what you're talking about."

Kiki looked at Pete and Mario for backup. "Just say what you mean," Mario said.

"I mean, I know, or I can imagine, I'm reading the signs that you feel vulnerable right now, like the world is out to get you."

"Not the world," Laurie said. "Just America."

"But that's what I'm saying. I wouldn't let anything bad happen to you. Neither would Dave. Neither would my kids, for that matter. But I don't think you'll need us. I promise you in four or eight years or whatever this will all be over and you'll be fine. You'll be better than fine."

"And you'll have four more kids," Sharmila said. She thought it would sound more jocular than it did. A smile froze on Kiki's face, and everyone else looked at Sharmila like she'd gone too far, like she'd made motherhood the enemy.

"Okay, I hope I haven't made a total fool of myself," Kiki said, and Sharmila, to make up for her flippant comment, told her to be careful on the walkway, realizing too late that anything she said now, even out of genuine concern for Kiki's safety, would sound sarcastic.

As soon as Kiki stepped outside, Laurie grabbed Sharmila's

hand and squeezed. They'd put off working on the front path because it was not an exciting renovation, but one day someone was going to fall and sue their asses. Thankfully, Kiki made it to the sidewalk and ran the rest of the way home.

After Laurie closed the door, Pete said, "That got weird."

"What do you think she was trying to say?" Sharmila asked. "That she voted for Trump?"

"I didn't get that," Mario said. "That's not what I got."

"She never said they *didn't* vote for Trump," Sharmila said. "Instead she lectured us on how lucky we are."

"That was some bullshit," Pete said.

Laurie was quiet for a few minutes. When she spoke again, it was an impersonation of Kiki saying *four or eight years or whatever,* and it was so uncanny they couldn't stop laughing. They didn't turn the TV back on, but stayed up late talking about Kiki's visit. They started going around in circles. Was disengaging a way of fighting, or was it just capitulation? Could they not feel the little gears clicking inside their consciences, making frequent, tiny adjustments until nothing was shocking or outrageous anymore? Were they right to be so afraid, or would they, in fact, be fine?

The next day felt especially melancholy. Pete and Mario were going back to the city where there were at least many diversions and the appearance of a robust world more immune to the vicissitudes of the rest of the country. Sharmila and Laurie did not feel so comfortable up in Ithaca, and three days later, when an Indian immigrant was shot dead in a Kansas bar, they wondered what to do, how much meaning they should cull from it. Then there were stabbings in May—a Black college student in Maryland and three white men defending Muslim girls in Portland.

Wanting to escape, Laurie and Sharmila left the country for the summer. They watched the riot in Charlottesville on French TV just days before their flight back to the US and they didn't want to come home, even to their friends or to the house they'd spent so much time fixing up.

But soon enough, the semester began and they were busy again. On a Saturday in September when the whole neighborhood seemed to be outside, Laurie and Sharmila went out to the porch with their cups of coffee. A landscaper was coming to show them some designs for their front lawn and walkway. From across their yards, the Catholics looked up from their chores and waved, and Laurie and Sharmila, feeling fine, waved back.

A Century Ends

It is decided at a staff meeting that *The End of the Century* will be the schoolwide theme, and since it would be a mathematical fallacy to celebrate the year 2000 as the start of the new millennium, they all have to agree that it is not the turn or dawn of anything yet, just the end. Ellora and Jane, both first grade teachers, have been passing notes back and forth with their own suggested titles for the schoolwide theme: *The Beginning of the End*; *A New Beginning Begins*; *The End of Something Followed by the Beginning of Something Else*; *Same Shit, Different Century*.

But sometime around Thanksgiving, Jane stops joking around. Without warning Ellora, she quits teaching to join a yoga instructor training program, and when Ellora asks her to explain, Jane can't explain, or doesn't want to, but invites Ellora to a women's spiritual retreat in Costa Rica over winter break. It's lucky that Ellora's parents are going to India in December, which means she doesn't have to go home to Ohio. She accepts the invitation in the hopes that she and Jane can reconnect and maybe even that it will feel like a vacation, the only true vacation she's ever taken over a winter break.

It almost feels like old times on the airplane. They pay extra for plastic cups of cheap chardonnay and laugh at all the same parts of the in-flight movie. When they walk out of the airport to catch a taxi, the heat is a pleasant shock. They have to stay in a community center in San José, nowhere near the coast or the water. All Ellora wants to do is drink piña coladas on a beach and maybe take a tour of the rainforest while Jane talks to her, opens up about the totality of what is going on with her.

They have to follow a strictly regimented schedule of lectures and community circles where they discuss their "knots." This is not at all relaxing. When it is Ellora's turn to reveal her primary knot, she says she doesn't have one.

The facilitator, a silver-haired woman with a whispery voice, encourages her to reach back into her dreams, memories, and family stories, because these knots, which one could think of as trauma, can be inherited from past generations and even from past lives. Except for Jane and Ellora, all the women are white. This is surprising because Jane, much more than Ellora, has expressed discomfort when they are the only minorities in the room, yet here she is in a country of brown people not only willingly surrounded by white people but immersed with them, participating in their project. At breakfast that morning, one of the women had asked Jane if she was raised a Buddhist, and when Jane told her they went to a Korean Presbyterian church, the woman lost interest and turned away. And Jane simply went on eating her breakfast without a hint of annoyance at the blatant orientalism.

"Reincarnation isn't real," Ellora says, "so I won't be reaching into that, but I guess I'm surprised the world hasn't ended. I'd say that's my knot." The women have learned how to probe the speaker for more, so Ellora starts recalling the disaster movies of her youth, which had convinced her that a nuclear war, a meteor strike, a pandemic, or something unforeseen would wipe them all out. As she talks, she realizes what a shame it is to spend so much of one's life fearing extinction-level events. The facilitator looks unsatisfied, but moves on.

Jane says her knot is that she always wanted to teach in a low-income urban school, but her body is rebelling against what her mind and heart wants. "This conflict inside of me is causing such pain, excruciating, physical pain. My jaw hurts. My back hurts. My feet hurt. The only relief I get is from yoga. But what do I do about my mind? What do I do about my heart?" This does not sound to Ellora like a knot. Just an excuse. Jane does not come from a wealthy background. She went to Yale on a full scholarship, but Jane's parents, unlike Ellora's, never put pressure on her to pursue a high-paying career, so this couldn't be about money. It isn't as if she'll make a fortune as a yoga teacher anyhow. There is some other internal pull, Ellora guesses. Maybe some guilt. Maybe Jane is afraid she won't be able to take care of her parents when they get older.

"Teaching makes the body hurt," Ellora says for the benefit of all the nonteachers in the room. Outsiders don't understand the physical energy required to manage a large group of young children all day long.

For the rest of the day, when it's time to do exercises with a partner, Jane grabs hold of someone else before Ellora can even locate her in the room. At dinner, which they eat at a long table, Jane doesn't sit anywhere near her. It's only when they are retiring for the night in their dorm room that Ellora has a chance to ask her what the hell is going on.

Jane is in her pajamas doing one more downward facing dog to stretch out her back. "You really don't know?"

"I don't. Please enlighten me."

"Why did you blurt out that thing about teaching making the body hurt?"

"Because it's true. I thought I was backing you up."

"No, Ell, you weren't backing me up. You took something I said that was specific to me and made it about every teacher in the whole world. You made me feel worthless."

Ellora apologizes. The last thing she wants is to make Jane feel worthless. "You're such a good teacher, Jane. Don't you think the job is getting easier now that we have some experience? Plus, I thought we had such a great summer. Most people don't get their summers off. I mean, has quitting teaching made you happy?"

Jane comes out of her pose and lies prostrate on the floor. She doesn't answer, and Ellora, thinking she has hit the right nerve, continues. "This is all so narcissistic. It just isn't you."

"Stop," Jane says. "You're making it worse."

Ellora stops, but she goes to bed bitter about how Jane's spiritual awakening has taken away her soul. This Jane is nothing like the woman she started teaching with three years ago. This Jane is the shell of a vibrant person who once lived in that body and cared about other people. Ellora cannot figure out how this transformation escaped her notice until it was too late, and if it has nothing or everything to do with her.

On the last day, December 29, they are guided through meditation and chanting to manifest world peace in the coming Age of Aquarius. Ellora always thought this was just a song from *Hair*, but no, it is an actual thing in astrology, a period of expanded consciousness when humanity finally takes control of its destiny, which this group of women has intuited will be coming with the new millennium. Before they finish, Ellora breaks the circle and walks out. She decides to wander around the art district and eat dinner on her own at a place full of locals. Jane would have liked this better. When Ellora gets back to the dorm room, Jane has left her a note saying she has taken an earlier flight out.

It was a terrible trip, but in the taxi heading back to her apartment in Brooklyn, Ellora misses the pastel colors of San José. New York looks gray and ugly, and all of its people miserable. On New Year's Eve she calls and leaves a message on Jane's answering machine, asking if she has plans for that night and if not, if she wants to go to a party or just come over and stay in and watch TV. Ellora knows that Jane is lonely, as lonely as Ellora.

Jane doesn't call back until the next day, when Ellora is hungover from getting drunk the night before, by herself, while watching premature celebrations of the new millennium sweep across the globe. "It was a mistake to take you to Costa Rica," Jane says. "I can't believe you walked out in the middle of the peace circle."

"Peace circle? Jane, those women are only concerned about their own comfort. World War III could be breaking out around them and they'd still be chanting."

"I can't see you anymore," Jane says. "I think you're my knot."

Ellora wonders if she could make Jane laugh by saying, "Not!"

"What did I do?" Ellora says. "What did I miss?"

"You keep asking me to explain myself to you but you're the one who won't talk, Ell. Your family treats you like shit and you think you don't have any knots? Come on, you act out your issues all the time including by trying to be fucking *teacher of the year*. Maybe I'm too focused on myself right now—I'll give you that—but you, God, it's like you don't even *have* a self."

Ellora doesn't appreciate the deflection. She still thinks her stories about her parents and two brothers are pretty funny. She remembers how horrified Jane was when she told her their nickname for her, roughly translated from the Bengali as *dummy*, and how after every trip home, when Ellora would describe to Jane their interactions and arguments, Jane would comment on how mean and abnormal it all seemed. Ellora's biggest problem with her family is not how they treat her but how they look at the rest of the world, with such certainty and arrogance, like nothing is ever complicated or layered or changeable. But Jane wants to pathologize something that Ellora has learned to cope with just fine. She moved halfway across the country and now rarely has to see them. She thinks about them less and less every year.

"You have nothing to say?" Jane prods.

"Just that you shouldn't have left your class in the middle of the year. You really fucked them up."

Jane actually chortles, the laugh she used to reserve for people they despised together. "You're not saving anyone," she says, and because Ellora hangs up immediately, these are the last words spoken between them.

On the first day back at school, Ellora uses a marker that smells like a blueberry lollipop to write the date at the top of the chart paper. January 4, 2000. All the zeros look strange to her. "This is the last year of the twentieth century," she says to her class. Although she has explained the word *century* multiple times, it's been a challenge for Ellora's first graders to understand the concept. The scale of time they are supposed to grasp eludes them.

"Ha ha, we're a hundred years old," Robbie says.

"The word century does have to do with the number one hundred," Ellora says, "but none of us here is one hundred years old."

Everyone starts calling out their ages. *I'm six. I'm seven. You're seven?* Ellora lets it go for a minute before giving them their assignment. "Write about how you will make the twenty-first century awesome." This sounds open-ended enough that they can take it in any direction they wish.

Ellora asks her students to put their thinking caps on. "What are some ideas you have for the next century—*your* century."

Someone yells out, "No school!" This naturally gets a lot of chuckles.

"No more drugs! No more fighting!" cries Maritza. Maritza's mother is in a halfway house trying to get her children back from foster care. They had one supervised visit scheduled for the holidays. Maritza was beside herself before the break, so worried that Y2K would ruin Christmas with her mother. Ellora reassured her by explaining in a kid-friendly version what Y2K was, and joking that everything should at least be okay until New Year's Day. Maritza understood both the joke and the reassurance.

Hoping Maritza's example will sink in with everyone, Ellora doesn't bother to solicit any more ideas and sends them to their tables to begin work. For the next ten minutes, it's so quiet that even her whispers of encouragement feel disruptive to the space they need. To resist the urge to hover over them, she looks out the windows of the south-facing wall. These kids don't know how lucky they are to have this view of Lower Manhattan. In different kinds of weather, she guides them to draw the scene out the window using only crayons—no pencils, no erasures. Whatever their eyes translate to their fingers is what goes on the paper. Her own artistic talents are regrettably limited, but she tries to show them what can happen when her eyes follow the lines. When she lets herself see the colors in the sky, she can create something memorable.

Against her will, her thoughts wander to Jane. They were both first-year teachers when they met. Ellora was introverted, prepared to keep her head down and hide in her classroom, but Jane, friendly and irreverent, pulled her into her orbit. She didn't realize until Jane left how isolating it could be in a classroom all day with small children. Having an adult friend at work, someone to laugh with, made Ellora a better teacher.

A commotion breaks out behind her. When Ellora turns around, Robbie is holding his neck and wheezing unnaturally, his face a sickening shade of purple and his eyes wild with panic. The kids at his table think he swallowed an eraser. Not the nubby ones at the ends of the pencils. The big pink ones that are so nice and oblong at the beginning of the year but stabbed by pencil points and butchered into useless pieces by the end of November. Ellora rushes over and holds his face in her hands. She peers into his open mouth to see if she can reach in and grab the eraser. She sees nothing but his tongue and his uvula and his tonsils and the dark caverns of his upper throat, and when she reaches in with her hooked finger it only seems to make things worse. Swallowing her own panic, she orders Maritza to run to the nurse's office while she slaps Robbie on the back as hard as she can. His wheezing gets louder.

All the teachers are trained in CPR as part of their certification, but Ellora hasn't committed any of it to muscle memory. She can only act out the Heimlich maneuver based on what she's seen on television. She puts her fist at the top of his belly, covering it with her other hand and thrusting. He feels as slight and bony as a bird. There's no give to his flesh and she keeps thinking that she's breaking him, breaking him and not saving him. This seems to go on forever, with no result.

Suddenly everything stops. His eyes close and his body goes limp in Ellora's arms. "No," she cries, laying him down on the floor. Where is Maritza and the nurse? She can't remember whether she's supposed to do mouth-to-mouth now or chest compressions. Behind her, the class is stomping and shouting, "Robbie's dead! Robbie's dead!" This might prompt someone from the hallway to come in and check on them, but stomping and chanting isn't unusual in Ellora's classroom.

She starts chest compressions but forgets to count them when at last Nurse Linda is at her side taking over. She tilts his head back and leans down to do a rescue breath, the step Ellora had missed. Ellora stands up and pushes her students toward the wall. She thinks of taking them out of the classroom, not wanting them to see Robbie fail to wake up. But something changes before she has to decide. The next time Nurse Linda opens Robbie's mouth, she's able to reach in and grab hold of the eraser, pulling it out swiftly and tossing it aside. It's covered in slime and for a moment almost looks like it's pulsing, like it's the still-beating heart of a small wounded animal. The kids start chanting, "Come on, Robbie, wake up, Robbie." Then Robbie's body heaves and revives with the most wonderful retching sound. Nurse Linda cradles his head, helping him to sit up. Ellora wonders why he isn't crying. She imagines he should be wailing like a newborn baby freeing the air in his lungs. The class is quiet at last, spellbound as Robbie slowly regains consciousness.

It's not much longer before EMS is there, followed by Helen, the principal, and Vicky, the social worker. The paramedic calls him *buddy* and asks him to respond to a few simple questions. Thank God Robbie still knows his name. They put him on the stretcher and carry him out as the kids sing, "Get better, Robbie. We love you, Robbie."

No one suggests that she go to the hospital with him. In the meantime, her class has refused to settle down. She doesn't want to yell at them after what just happened, but if she doesn't get them under control, she will lose her mind. She grabs a tissue and picks up the offending eraser. Then she shakes her tambourine and gives them twenty seconds to clean up their tables. She has to kill fifteen minutes before it's time to line up for art class.

She gathers them on the rug for "Jump Jim Joe." The words of the song tell them what to do.

> Jump, jump, jump Jim Joe.
> Shake your head and nod your head and tap your toe.
> Around and around and around we go
> And we make a great big circle and we jump Jim Joe.

At the end of the song they have to plop into their places in the circle. They cooperate because they know it's time to play a game. She reaches into the basket behind her to grab the ball that they'll roll to each other—no one can receive the ball twice. It's a regular-size gym ball, but this one looks like the earth. She rolls it to David, who rolls it to Juanito, who rolls it to Dylan. Ellora clears her throat. "Dylan, I want you to pause and think for a minute. Can you roll the ball to someone you don't get to talk to very often?" He looks around, and then rolls it to a girl, Marion, who is so quiet it's easy for everyone to forget about her. The smile on Marion's face when the ball comes to her moves Ellora in a way she doesn't expect. She fights back tears as she watches the earth roll across the carpet, the oceans and continents and melting polar ice caps landing in her students' doughy hands for a few seconds at a time.

When the ball rolls back to her, fat tears are streaming down her cheeks. No one says anything. No one starts sniffling or crying with her either. Sometimes if one student hurts another's feelings, she will let her eyes water for effect as she lectures the class about kindness. She always considers it a success if some of the students cry with her. But this time they do not dare to mimic her. They must think that she's crying about Robbie, because he almost died and they were all a witness to it. The only reaction is from Maritza, sitting next to her, who puts her little hand in Ellora's.

While the kids are in art class, she goes to the office and fills out the incident form. The social worker has called in from the emergency room. They are keeping Robbie for observation but so far, he's doing fine. The secretary looks at Ellora and asks her if she wants to go home early. Ellora shakes her head. She isn't so weak that she would leave her students, and what would she do at home anyway?

Of course, word gets around school that Robbie had to be taken to the hospital. In the cafeteria, his kindergarten teacher says it was only a matter of time before he choked on something. The subtext is not hard to read. Other teachers, as soon as they see her, give her hugs before they ask for more details—the gossip—about what happened. This is the part that makes Ellora do something unprecedented. As soon as her last student is picked up, she gathers her things and leaves.

She stops at her favorite dive bar for a drink and has dinner by herself at a trendy new Italian restaurant on 8th Street. She used to do this with Jane. Because they were both single when everyone else had partners and children to run home to, they went out a lot after work, trying all the new bistros popping up on the way to the subway station. They started calling Avenue B, Avenue Bistro.

By the time she gets home, she feels both numb and slightly delirious. There are no messages on her answering machine. It's not even nine o'clock yet but she gets under the covers and thinks that if she calls Jane and tells her what happened to Robbie, it would be a surrender, an admission that Jane is right about the answers to real problems being found in navel-gazing or fantastical flights of the imagination. Jane will say the eraser getting stuck in Robbie's throat is no coincidence. She will turn it into some kind of metaphor, or worse, a sign that the universe is trying to get through to her. And Ellora, feeling exhausted, might admit that she failed to retrieve the knot, failed to save Robbie's life, maybe even allowing that it was due to divine mercy, not Nurse Linda, that he didn't die. Ellora is the one who is worthless. Who is she kidding, thinking she can save a whole generation?

She tries to imagine the peace and forgiveness on Jane's face if Ellora concedes. She tries to remember what Jane looked like before the universe made her so certain of everything. Ellora sleeps fitfully, and in her dreams, Robbie does not wake up. Her parents and brothers are at the funeral, laughing at her.

Yet Robbie is back at school the very next day. At first his classmates heap all their attention on him, and during the morning meeting, Ellora gives him a chance to tell them about his trip to the hospital. He says the doctors looked in his brain, which brings up all kinds of questions Robbie can't answer, but after an hour of school, yesterday's incident is all but forgotten. Ellora has removed the erasers from the tables and keeps a close eye on

Robbie, resisting the temptation to lift his chin and make him open his mouth every few minutes.

They have to finish their writing assignment on how they would make the next century awesome. It's becoming apparent that Ellora has neglected the schoolwide theme all year and it's time to put something on display. Most of the students only worked on their drawings and have not written a sentence yet. She pushes them harder today, walking around and asking them what they plan to do next. And since there are no interruptions, it turns out to be a productive session. When she calls the kids back to the rug and asks who wants to share, they all raise their hands. "I don't know if we'll get to all of you, but let's start with Robbie."

Robbie reads what he wrote. "When I am a hundred years old, I will still love Miss Ellora. I will take care of her because she will be two hundred years old!"

He didn't understand the assignment, but what did it matter? He took a marvelous mental trip into the future and came back with this amazing declaration. The whole class claps for him, and Ellora feels a newfound confidence. How wrong Jane is. How wrong she is about everything.

Ellora can see her class performing a skit on the stage in which they push the metaphorical barrel of the twentieth century, with all its progress and horrors, to the cusp of the next millennium. There they will open it up, holding up objects that represent the good things they want to keep and the bad things they will leave behind, before they cross the threshold into a new age. When she was young, she was not taught to question what was given to her. This script, that they will write together, can change the world. The kids will never forget it.

A New Race of Men
from Heaven

I decided to seek counseling because I wanted to sleep with a man from my office, an engineer with hazel eyes and auburn hair cut close to his scalp, a slightly receding chin and a quite large nose, and one dimple, in his left cheek, when he smiled. He came to us from Glasgow to manage the electrical component of the Heathrow Terminal Five project. Every time he stopped by the finance department he would hover by my desk and engage me in suggestive banter. Once I said, "I'll have the report run by the end of the day. Be sure to grab me before you leave," and he said, "I will, I'll grab you," and we both laughed.

I wondered if he was married, and discovered, by procuring his personnel file from a temporary admin assistant in HR, that Ned was not married. He was only horrendously busy with the electrical infrastructure of the Heathrow project. We'd been flirting harmlessly all those months until the day he began talking about Palms of Goa, an Indian restaurant on Charlotte Street close to our office. He was asking me to lunch.

"I don't like Indian restaurants," I blurted. I shook my head and tried to recover. "You're thinking this must be some kind of racial self-hatred. The truth is my mother is English, and my father died when I was sixteen."

"It doesn't have to be Indian," he said.

I wanted to clarify that I disliked Indian restaurants, not Indian food, and certainly not Indian people. "We went to an Indian restaurant for my tenth birthday. It didn't go well. My mother said the food was too spicy and she fussed at the waiter."

"We mustn't recreate bad childhood memories," he said.

"One of my best mates is Kashmiri. I've had lovely meals with her family."

He nodded wearily. "Italian then?"

"I can't," I said. I had meant to say *today. I can't today.* I needed a little time, a day or two, to prepare for a lunch with him.

He backed away from my desk, undoing his strident approach. I almost cried watching him retreat.

After that, his avoidance of me was brutal.

I chose my counselor, Nicole, because she looked energetic and kept a tidy office, and because, like myself, she was of mixed parentage—a Jamaican father and Welsh mother. She listened to my story about Ned and asked, "Why didn't you go to lunch with him?"

That's when I told her I had never been with a man. I was twenty-eight years old and a virgin. Nicole looked at me with a kind of greedy sympathy before asking me about my relationship with my father. I was not so naive to think that sexual problems in adult women would not be connected back to the father. I was prepared and eager to talk about him. "He died. Cancer. When I was sixteen. I have happy memories of him."

I waited for her to ask another question. She waited for me to continue.

"He was from India, as you know." From my detailed recounting of Ned's failure to take me to Indian for lunch. "He was a nice man. Hardworking. There was nothing very complicated about him. He loved sightseeing."

Nicole smiled. She asked me to tell a story about him, something I remembered.

"Well, this is funny. I didn't know he was from India until I was nine years old!" I knew she wasn't looking for entertainment, but I didn't want to be boring.

It was 1987, and Dad and I had just walked from the British Museum to Piccadilly Circus on one of our frequent father-daughter excursions to London. It was a warm, gray day in summer, no rain. We were sitting on the steps by the statue of Eros, watching the traffic circling and the tourists aiming their cameras at the curved neon adverts for Fujifilm and Sanyo. My feet were tired from walking. I linked my arm through my father's and leaned heavily against him, perfectly tranquil.

In Piccadilly, the tourists conversed in different languages—German, French, Japanese, Swedish. Suddenly I heard a sharp nasal voice close by, speaking an unfamiliar language. I sat up and saw my father looking to his left at an elderly man standing there.

The man wore a maroon turban, as well as a pair of ridiculously thick glasses that magnified his round eyes. A large boxy Nikon camera hung from a strap around his neck. He was so top-heavy I was afraid he would teeter over and fall into my father's lap. My father and the man were talking to each other, but in their conversation, the man seemed to have cast a spell over my father, unspooling from his throat a language I could not name. The words came out fast, as if he did not have to think about them first. I watched my father turn younger, sitting with his hands on his knees, and I realized this was my father before I existed. For the length of their conversation, I was alone, orphaned in Piccadilly. I tugged on Dad's sleeve three or four times before he noticed me. "I have to go to the loo," I lied. He looked around, past me, as if he were hoping to find my real guardian.

I squeezed my legs together and squirmed as if I were about to wet myself. My father, embarrassed, stood up and made some kind of apology, and we walked hand in hand into Lillywhites, where I pretended to find the toilet and take a wee while he looked at cricket bats.

He was sullen during most of the tube ride home. I looked around at all the passengers standing shoulder to shoulder, their bodies swaying with the pitch of the train. My father did not resemble any of the English men, nor did he resemble the darker-skinned Asians, and I imagined him to be entirely unique, a race unto himself.

I put my hand in his. "Did you know that man?" I asked him.

He seemed to warm to my company again. "No. We come from the same region in India."

It was the first time he told me he came from India. I suppose he'd never had a reason to tell me before, or else he thought I knew, as I should have by that age.

"How did *he* know that? You don't wear a turban."

"We can tell, sometimes. And I looked at him. I nodded my head."

I didn't understand.

"Will we go to India?" I asked.

"No," he said, looking away. He didn't explain, and I knew never to ask him again.

Before he died my father forgot his English altogether. From his deathbed, he spoke to us as if we ought to have understood, and when we didn't, when our English frightened and angered him, we couldn't guess what ugly things he said to us in his mother tongue. The hardest thing about watching my father die was his sudden ill temper, his foreign rage. He didn't seem to recognize me at all, not until the last time we were alone. Still speaking Punjabi, he grasped a lock of my hair and said something that sounded like a nursery rhyme. I sometimes wish I had recorded him, tried harder to understand what he was saying.

Nicole was frowning. "It doesn't seem like you could properly say goodbye. You were speaking two different languages, weren't you?"

I began to cry. I adored my father. I could still feel the prickliness of his mustache on my fingers and his stubble on my lips and once I wanted nothing more than to grow up and marry him. He had black eyes and a steady gaze that was warm and fervid, obliterating, but who would say that to their counselor, a perfect stranger?

CHAITALI SEN

"You've done very well, Sasha. I applaud you for taking this step." I was startled that we were out of time. *What about Ned?* I wanted to say, but I would have to wait until next time. I wanted her to understand that I was there to solve this virginity that was destroying my life. I had even started avoiding my mates, who were all coupling up and getting married. None of them had any idea that I was a virgin. I made it sound as if I had a freewheeling sex life that was too exciting to discuss, lest it make them feel bad about their dull boyfriends. But even they were starting to get bored with this routine.

A few weeks later, I was having tea with my mother in the back garden of my childhood home in Hornchurch. Over slices of strawberry tart, she reprised her adventures at Lloyds where she had been a teller for twelve years, since my father died. Her stories were amusing. She told them with animated gestures, her blue eyes flitting and lively. Occasionally she brushed her long chestnut bangs away from her brow. When I was very young, my hair was the same color as hers.

In one of my sessions with Nicole, I'd said something unkind about my mother, about how she used her Englishness as an advantage in her marriage. To my surprise, Nicole asked me what I meant by that. I assumed she would understand, that something about this would feel true to her, but then again, her mother was Welsh, not English.

When my mother was finished with her tales and asked what was new with me, I told her I'd started counseling.

She was startled. "Psychotherapy? Whatever for?"

158

"I've had some issues."

"But they can't be serious. I think you've turned out quite all right."

"Thanks, Mum. It's just . . . have you never wondered about my love life? You never ask."

"That's your business. It's not as if I'm desperate for a grand-child." For some reason, this made her laugh heartily.

I was determined to continue. "Were you happy with Dad?"

My mother shook her finger in the air. "Ah, I know what you're up to. *I* don't need counseling, darling."

"I wasn't suggesting you did. I was just trying to discuss some-thing with you. About Dad."

"Don't tell me he molested you."

"Oh my God, Mum."

"It's a fad among young women these days to accuse their fathers of molestation. Makes them feel part of a club of some sort."

"I'm not that young, Mum."

"It happened to Jeremy Smalls from up the street. Do you remem-ber him? He adored his daughter and she turned against him."

"Jeremy Smalls was a creep," I said. "Don't you want to know what I talk about in counseling?"

"Your love life, obviously, since you brought it up."

"Mum, I didn't know about Dad's cancer until he was too sick to hide it," I said, which was true. "You should have told me sooner. I think Dad felt very alone when he died. I think he missed his family in India. I would have liked to ask him some more things when he was lucid, about his childhood, about my heritage."

"Don't be daft, Sasha. Your heritage is right here in England. He didn't have any family in India."

"That can't be true, Mum."

"Of course it's true. He was estranged from them. *We* were his family."

She often talked about their courtship as if they were orphans who'd rescued each other. When they met, she was sitting on a bench in Hyde Park, forlorn about a boy she'd left behind in Colchester. My father appeared and asked if he could take her picture, and then they walked for hours, and then they were inseparable. She had the photograph as proof, the first of many flattering portraits my father took of her.

I used to hate that I didn't look like her, especially after the numerous times people remarked they could see none of my mother in me. When I was thirteen, I had a growth spurt, and all of my features became more extreme—my nose wider, my eyebrows thicker, my hair and eyes almost as black as my father's. My somewhat masculine look made me feel so insecure and unattractive that I started to avoid being seen with my mother, just to spare me the misery. Only when I walked down the street with my father, unmistakably his daughter, did I experience any kind of self-confidence.

"You're missing the point," I said. "Don't you remember how it was at the end? How he wouldn't speak English?"

"What are you talking about?"

"He spoke only Punjabi when he was dying."

My mother scoffed.

"He did, Mum!"

She insisted that I was wrong, and there was no point in arguing. I stared at her, with rage at first, but she looked so miserable, so determined to remain true to her delusion, that I ended up feeling only pity.

I changed the subject. She asked me how my work was going. There was nothing remarkable to report there, so I told her about Ned. Perhaps my mother had some good advice for me.

"Office romances can be tricky," she said, "but if you like him enough, go for it!" She then went on to tell me again about her friend Poppy, who'd had a disastrous affair with her boss many years ago. One should know that, with Poppy, everything was a disaster.

The next time I saw Nicole I had good news for her. My engineer and I were friends again. He'd asked, "Are you all right, Sasha?" and I'd said, "Yes, I'm fine," and then we started laughing at the formality of it all.

Nicole was not as enamored with the story as I was.

"Sasha, what do you want from this man?"

"What do you mean?"

"Do you want to sleep with him? Do you want a relationship? Do you want something that doesn't go any further than the office?"

"Yes, I want to sleep with him," I said.

"Is that all?"

"No. I want to go to the market with him." I find food shopping very mundane, and my idea of domestic bliss is strolling down the market aisles and filling the cart up while someone I love amuses me.

"So, you want a relationship with him. You want to become intimate."

"I think *Ned and Sasha* has a nice ring to it. We would be Ned and Sasha."

Nicole liked this. "If that's what you want, that's wonderful. What do you think is different about Ned?" I knew what she was getting at. In our previous session, she had asked me about my experiences with dating, from university onward. I told her about all the boys who had chased me, with no luck, not to boast but to prove that my virginity was not from a lack of opportunity.

"I don't know. He's confident. He's funny. He's successful."

"And available?"

I assured her that he was, confessing how I had snuck into his personnel file. Nicole did not disapprove of this in the least. She was very glad to hear that he was unmarried, and that I had chosen a man with whom a commitment was a real possibility.

All in all, it helped to talk to someone about my life. I was starting to feel lighter, freer. The following week, I floated confidently through a maze of desks on the engineering floor and landed in Ned's little office. He stood up as soon as he saw me and waited for me to say something. I was holding a stack of purchase orders for him to sign, but I'd forgotten all about them. "I'm available for lunch today," I said.

His eyebrows shot up, then collapsed again. "I can't today. We have the rail meeting. It's going to be hell."

"Oh."

"What about dinner?" he asked.

"Dinner?" I had my counseling session. I hated to cancel. "I have an appointment at five-thirty, in Greenwich."

"Greenwich? Is that where you live? I could come meet you there."

He lived in North London, in Stoke Newington. I wasn't meant to know that but of course I did know, his exact street address in fact. It wasn't an impossible distance, but on a weeknight, after dinner and a few glasses of wine, it was far enough.

"You could come by my flat," I said. "We could get some Chinese takeaway, or I could cook."

"You don't know how brilliant that sounds."

We traded papers—my address and mobile number for the signed invoices—and we finalized our plan. He would come around eight.

Nicole could see I was excited about my date. If I had any anxiety about it, it didn't come to the surface, so she asked me easy questions about what I was going to cook, what I was going to wear, and so on. There was no point in dragging out the session. She said, "You deserve to be happy," and sent me on my way.

Ned was very punctual, showing up at my door at exactly eight o'clock. He was standing there holding a bottle of wine, still in his work clothes, with his tie on but no jacket. I had on a black dress and wore my hair down. He looked at my hair, at my dress, and said, "You look nice," but his gaze was more expressive than his language. I stepped aside and let him in.

As I showed him around my flat, he admired the décor and kissed me once in the doorway of the bedroom. I pulled away smiling, happy to get that over with, then took his hand and led him to the kitchen. We talked while I made dinner, a simple pasta with olive oil and vegetables, and he opened the bottle of wine he'd brought. He said he'd never been to Greenwich. He had expected to have more leisure time, but this Heathrow project was all-consuming.

"Maybe when the project is over," he said, "you can be my tour guide."

"I'm uniquely qualified," I said. I told him about my childhood spent exploring London, and how I first discovered Greenwich with my father when I was thirteen. There was so much to see here, the Royal Observatory, Greenwich Park, and the Old Royal Naval College with its two domes, its perfect symmetry. I recounted our visit to the Painted Hall, where we wandered for hours under the frescoed ceiling and the gilded arch, gods and angels everywhere. My father had told me it took nineteen years to complete, and when it was finished, it was deemed too grand for its original purpose as a dining hall. He had read aloud the translations of the Latin inscriptions. There was one in particular that always stayed with me. It was from the west wall depicting the arrival of the House of Hanover. *A new race of men from heaven*, my father read.

Ned looked fascinated. "Was your father a professor? A historian?"

I laughed. "No, nothing that interesting. He was a chemist." I did not feel compelled to add that I hadn't been back to the Painted Hall since visiting with my father, despite living so close to the Royal Naval College. I imagined going there with Ned. It would be the first stop on our tour.

We ate at my small kitchen table by the window and talked more about places, about London and Glasgow and about a wedding he'd gone to in India where the actual ceremony didn't take place until two in the morning because the time was set by the astrologer.

"My father never talked about India," I said.

Ned seemed to understand. "It's not the easiest of places."

After dinner, we cleaned up the dishes and sat on the sofa with our wine. I asked him about his family, his parents. He told me they were nice people, divorced.

"And you've never been married?" I asked.

"No. I came close. I was with someone for ten years. We got engaged. Planned a wedding. Sent out the invitations. One day, before it was too late, we realized we were getting married instead of splitting up, which was what we were meant to do."

I was surprised. "You canceled the wedding?"

"We did. She's happily married to someone else now."

"It's very brave," I said. "Most people would have gone on and done it rather than face the shame."

"We disappointed a lot of people. Some of them still don't talk to us."

"Us? You're still friends?"

"Of course. We were always friends more than anything else."

"How wonderful."

Then he kissed me.

I was happy, of course. I grabbed his collar and put my lips all over the sandy surface of his jaw. Things escalated quickly, and after a while I could feel his stony erection. It is amazing how powerful men are despite this vulnerable appendage. Their arousal or lack of it is always so apparent, no bluffing, no deception. I took his tie off and whispered in his ear. "Will you stay, Ned?"

He put me on my back and kissed my neck and collarbone. When he moved down my body to the inside of my thighs, my thoughts started to race. I was relieved that it was going well, naturally, and that it was all finally happening for me, but I wondered what would come afterward. Would Ned be my boyfriend? Would he stay in London? Would I have to move to Glasgow? Would my mother like him? It troubled me that I had no idea how my mother might behave around him, and what he would think of her. He asked me, "Is this all right?" and I said, "Yes, yes," and he continued, pulling off my underwear and unzipping his trousers and parting my legs with his groin. He was heavier than I expected, but I enjoyed it, his manly heft.

"Condom," he said. "In my wallet."

I pulled his wallet out of his pocket. I watched him fumble for the square foil packet and tear it open with his teeth.

"Wait," I said.

I pushed his chest lightly, and he shifted so that I could move out from under him. I sat up and folded my legs. He sat up as well, looking alarmed at the way my body closed up so suddenly. It hit me then, the cost of my impatience. Everything that had come to me could be lost in an instant.

"I've never done this before," I said.

He thought he understood. "Because we work together? I've

never done it either, but we're adults. I like you very much, Sasha. Do you think it's a mistake?"

"No, I mean . . ."

I didn't know how to say it. I pointed to his erection. "That."

He was confused. Then he grinned. "I see," he said, nodding. "Women are much more fluid about their sexuality, aren't they? Especially, your age, younger women." He cleared his throat. "The younger generation." He winced, and I stopped him.

"It's not that. I'm not attracted to women," I said. "It's just that I had so many conditions, and none of those conditions have been met until now."

"That's . . . well . . . you flatter me."

"I shouldn't have put you in this position," I said. "I'm so embarrassed."

His hand moved to my knee. "Don't be embarrassed," he said. "You have nothing to be embarrassed about. I can only imagine how many poor hearts you've broken along the way."

I moved closer to him. He was so lovely.

"Do you want this?" he asked.

"Yes, more than anything, but it doesn't have to be tonight."

He kissed my hand gallantly. Then my wrist.

Soon we were lying on the sofa again and carrying on as we were. It was all going fine until he put his hand between my legs and caressed me with his thumb, and we both became aware at the same time that I was sobbing. He tried to kiss my tears away and make soft cooing sounds to soothe me, but I couldn't stop, I couldn't breathe.

"I miss my father. Do you want to be my father?"

He pulled away, looking startled and helpless and, in spite of it all, somewhat paternal. "My God, Sasha, what happened to you?"

I covered my face and made a sound I didn't think could have come from my own body. He stayed for a little while, but he didn't dare touch me again. When he spoke, he was very kind. "I don't think I can take this on right now." I curled up and turned my back to him. I listened as he put on his shoes, fixed his clothes, shut the door gently behind him.

After a while, with the help of a Valium I fell asleep, but in the middle of the night, I woke up convinced that my father was in the room with me. I could hear his footsteps, smell his wool coat, hear him whispering my name. In the seconds it took me to come fully to consciousness, I had never been so frightened, too frightened to even sit up and turn the light on. When the sun came up and filled the room, my fear turned to anger. I wished that I could let my father go. I wished that I could sleep with Ned. I wished that I could marry him and have children and live a long happy life. I could not understand why the things I wanted, which seemed to come easily to everyone else, were so beyond my abilities.

At our next appointment, I told Nicole everything about my date with Ned. Everything except for the feeling that my father was haunting me. If I tried to explain it to her, it would have opened up a line of questioning I knew wasn't necessary. It was simply that my father was everywhere, all the time. He was in the Painted Hall, in Greenwich Park, in Piccadilly. Perhaps when Ned was trying to make love to me, I was somewhere else, sitting close to my father, leaning my head on his shoulder, basking in a kind of love that was taken from me long before I was ready. Until he died, my father's side was the only place where I felt truly at home.

"You wanted to stop it from going any further. Why is that?" Nicole asked.

"I just don't know," I said. It was no use. I had nothing to offer.

When our time was up, she stood across from me and clasped my hands. "I'm here whenever you need me," she said. She must have known I would never go back.

I managed to avoid Ned until his phase of the Heathrow project ended and he went back to Glasgow. I imagined cornering him at his farewell party and kissing him goodbye. I imagined telling him not to go, and at night, I used this fantasy to masturbate to the point of orgasm. After doing that enough times, actual penetration didn't feel that far off. I ended up losing my virginity to a bloke in an Arsenal jersey.

Eventually, I met a man very unlike Ned, married him and had children. After a while I didn't know why I'd made such a fuss in my twenties. In my thirties, my mind became blissfully uncomplicated.

But much later, after my mother herself was diagnosed with cancer, she told me something that would have mattered long ago. I had temporarily moved her into our home in London during her treatments. With two young children, it was difficult for me to make frequent trips to Hornchurch to look after her, and I couldn't bear the thought of her being sick in that house where my father had not recovered. It was a good decision. She loved being pampered by me and entertained by the children.

On one of her worst mornings, when she asked me to stop what I was doing and sit with her, I said, "Mum, you're going to be fine." But she took my hand and held me captive there.

"I always expected to have a glamorous life," she said.

"What do you mean?" I asked, encouraging her to keep talking, to take her mind off the nausea.

"I had the looks to be an actress or model."

I agreed. It was why she had come to London, to be discovered. I knew this story already. At the part where she'd talk about how she met my father instead, I was meant to take this as the better ending. But this time, she confessed to me that on their first walk in Hyde Park, he told her he had a wife and young daughter in India who were waiting to join him in England. She invited him back to her room anyway.

She squeezed my hand tighter as she explained all this, though I could have easily escaped her still-feeble grip. I didn't think I had heard wrong; I didn't have to ask her to repeat herself. As soon as she spoke of the wife and daughter he'd left behind, I had no doubt of their existence.

She went on about how she'd wanted to tell me sooner, but she had promised my father that I would never know. Whether or not this was true, her struggle failed to move me. I was back at my father's deathbed, my palm absorbing the chill of his bony hand as it held on to a lock of my hair. The rhyme he recited, the adoration and sorrow in his last gaze upon my face, none of it had been for me. I remembered how he kept mispronouncing my name. Sa, Sa, Sai, Saila, Saila, Sailaja, Sailaja, Sailaja. A girl's name, but not mine.

I only asked my mother one question. "What language was Dad speaking when he died?"

"Punjabi?" she asked herself, as if she couldn't remember where he came from. "Yes, I believe it was Punjabi." She seemed to have no recollection of that time in her garden, when she could have said something, anything to assure me that the weight I had been feeling was real, even if it was not what I thought it was.

I'd never seen my mother so vulnerable, but I looked at her coldly.

"I didn't want to take this secret to my grave," she said.

"You're not dying, Mother."

She turned away from me. "You don't know how I suffered. I asked him to stay, and it was the last thing I ever got from him." In the end, causing a man to leave his family was the only remarkable thing she'd ever done. She was pretty, an English rose, and my father loved England.

My mother recovered and we never mentioned it again. But I kept wondering what would have changed if she hadn't waited so long to tell me the truth. I scrolled through various scenarios that were still possible. I imagined dropping by Nicole's office, or sending an email to Ned, whose movements I still managed to track from Glasgow to Beijing to New York. I spent some time looking up flights to Chandigarh, thinking about finding my sister. Invariably I was interrupted by my children, my adorably ferocious tyrants. When I showed them pictures of their grandfather, we could see what was always there, the greatness of the effort, the constant clenching of his heart.

Acknowledgments

These stories were developed over many years and with the help and support of many people. I can't express enough gratitude to all of my writing companions who have given me valuable feedback: Amin Ahmad, Sharbari Zohra Ahmed, Dena Afrasiabi, Jessica Bacal, Jo Ann Heydron, Donna Johnson, Swati Khurana, Ed Latson, Elizabeth Shah-Hosseini, Rose Smith, S. Kirk Walsh, and Kirk Wilson. I am eternally grateful to my agent, Betsy Lerner, for connecting so thoughtfully with my work and understanding how to make it better, and to the editors of the literary magazines that first published these stories: Steven Schwartz at *Colorado Review*, Richard Santos at *Front Porch Journal*, Christine Hyung-Oak Lee at *Kartika Review*, Anna Lena Phillips Bell at *Ecotone*, Beth Staples at *Ecotone* and *Shenandoah*, Patti Wisland at *New Ohio Review*, and Adeena Reitberger and Adam Soto at *American Short Fiction*. Literary magazines are essential to the vibrancy of our culture and they deserve all our support.

For all of their love, understanding, and encouragement, big hugs and thanks to Dalia Azim, Jude Benham and the entire

Benham family, Gouri Datta, Amit Dhar, Shari Getz, Charly Green, Jen Henderson, Adam Hettler, Seela Misra, Soyinka Rahim, Praba Reddy, Nandini Datta Roy, Niru Somasundaram, and so many family and friends from across the country and the globe.

It is especially meaningful to me that this collection was selected by contest judge Danielle Evans, whose work has been a touchstone for me. I can only aspire to become half the writer she is. It was a pleasure to work with the whole team at Sarabande Books, beginning with my brilliant editor, Kristen Miller. Thank you to Kristen, Sarah, Joanna, and Danika for holding my hand and bringing this book into the world.

This collection is dedicated to my mother Bharati Sen, my sister Rinku Sen, and my father Arun Sen, who always encouraged me to develop my imagination and put it to good use. I don't know who I would have become without them.

And all my love to Scott Benham, who lightens the load and inspires me every day.

ACKNOWLEDGMENTS

"The Immigrant" first appeared in *Colorado Review*

"When I Heard the Learn'd Astronomer" first appeared
in *Ecotone*

"The Matchstick, by Charles Tilly" first appeared in *Front
Porch Journal*

"Uma" first appeared in *Kartika Review*

"North, South, East, West" first appeared as "The Abandoned"
in *New Ohio Review*

"A Century Ends" first appeared in *American Short Fiction
Online*

"A New Race of Men from Heaven" first appeared
in *Shenandoah*

CHAITALI SEN's short stories and essays have appeared in *Boulevard, Colorado Review, Ecotone, Electric Literature, New England Review, Shenandoah*, and many other publications. She is the author of the novel *The Pathless Sky* and holds an M.F.A from Hunter College. Born in India and raised in the U.S., she currently lives in Texas with her family.

SARABANDE BOOKS is a nonprofit literary press located in Louisville, KY. Founded in 1994 to champion poetry, short fiction, and essay, we are committed to creating lasting editions that honor exceptional writing. For more information, please visit sarabandebooks.org.